A Shallow River of Mercy

by

Robert Hays

A Shallow River of Mercy

Copyright 2017 Robert Hays

Published by Thomas-Jacob Publishing, LLC

TJPub@thomas-jacobpublishing.com

Library of Congress Control Number: 2017957935
1. Contemporary fiction 2. Literary fiction
ISBN-13: 978-0-9979517-3-8
ISBN-10: 0-9979517-3-7
Thomas-Jacob Publishing, LLC, Deltona, FL USA

"I shall tell you a great secret, my friend. Do not wait
for the last judgment. It takes place every day."
                                    —Albert Camus, *La Chute*

To Earl and Margaret and precious memories

ONE

THE MAN SWUNG down from the high cab, on the passenger side, careful to keep a tight grip on the paper bag he carried in his right hand. His legs were stiff from the long ride and sharp pain shot through his bad knee as he dropped onto the hard surface of the potholed gravel parking lot. He waved goodbye with his free hand and shouted his thanks to the driver, hoping to make himself heard over the noisy clatter of the idling diesel engine, then covered his mouth and nose to protect against the swirl of choking dust and exhaust fumes left by the truck as it lumbered back onto the highway interchange.

The bone-chilling cold of an early Michigan winter cut through the man's light jacket and stung the exposed skin of his face and hands. The man, whose name was Ernst Kohl, was tall and thin and walked with a slight limp. His breath left little clouds of vapor in the frigid night air. He hurried toward the truck stop's restaurant, identified in large red neon lettering as the Purple Onion Grill. A smaller, flashing blue sign in a front window said "Breakfast any time." Breakfast was of no particular interest just now, but the grill would be warm. He pushed open the door and went in, unsure what to expect.

The dining room was dimly lit. An Italian movie with subtitles played on a wide-screen television set mounted on one wall, its sound muted. Kohl paused and looked about the room, then made his way somewhat hesitantly to the back and took a seat on a round, padded stool and stowed the paper bag on the floor between his feet. He rubbed his hands together to combat the cold and leaned forward with his elbows on the worn Formica counter.

A lone fry-cook seared hamburger patties on the griddle and didn't look at him at first, and then when he did he said, "They let you out, Kohl? It's been a few years, ain't it?"

"Yeah," Kohl said, "they let me out and it's been a few years. You goin' to get me something or not?"

The fry-cook waved off his question with a blackened metal spatula. "Hold your horses," he grumbled. "I ain't got but two hands. Anyway, whadaya want?"

Kohl shrugged his shoulders. "I don't know," he said. "Anything that's hot."

"Coffee's hot. Want some?"

"Yeah, sure. Give me a cup of coffee."

"You want something to eat?"

"That meat smells good."

The fry-cook laughed. He was a fat man and his laugh rumbled up from his big belly, rolled across the griddle against the stainless steel splash panel, and bounced back toward the seated customer. "Bet anything I make for you's better than what you been used to," he said. "Or maybe they put a little prime rib on the menu up there and I never heard about it."

Kohl ignored the sarcastic remark. He didn't say anything until the fat man set a cup and saucer in front of him and filled the cup with coffee. "Thanks," he mumbled then, and went about adding sugar and an artificial creamer to the dark brew and stirring vigorously with a spoon. The coffee was hot and it tasted good. He drank the whole cupful and looked back at the fry-cook and pushed his cup and saucer forward.

"Want some more?" the fry-cook asked.

"Yeah, I could use another cup. Do I know you?"

"You used to. I'm Danny Connor."

"It's been twenty years, Danny."

"If you say so." Danny Connor poured more coffee. "I'll fix you a hamburger, on the house. Soon as I take care of them truckers." He motioned with a nod of his head toward two men at a table near the front door. "One of 'em's my buddy, Tay."

Danny Connor carried hamburgers to the two truckers and poured more coffee for them. Kohl turned and watched. One of the truckers, a husky black man with a merry expression on his face and a wide smile, shook the fry-cook's hand and commenced an animated conversation. Danny Connor quaked with laughter, but motioned toward the back as if saying he had to get back to work. He was still laughing when he paused beside a tired-looking old man who sat alone at a table alongside the wall and studied a bowl of chili as if uncertain it was fit to eat. The old man looked up and shook his head no, and Danny hurried back to his station at the griddle. He finished cooking Kohl's hamburger and brought it on a wide white china platter with stacks of French fries and onion rings and stood in front of Kohl to see if he wanted anything else.

"This looks real good," Kohl said. "Sorry I didn't recognize you."

"Forget it. I'm twenty years older and a hundred pounds or so bigger than I was the last time you saw me. Anybody know you're coming?"

"Nobody left to tell," Kohl said. "Leastwise nobody who'd care."

"You goin' back to the old home place out on Old Church Road?"

"I'll go check it out and see what happens."

Kohl had never known Danny Connor well. He remembered when they both went to the same high school and Danny played football and Kohl wanted to play but wasn't good enough. Kohl's mother was still alive then. He was disappointed when he didn't make the team and needed her sympathy, but she said it was just as well because if he played football he'd probably go around the rest of his life on gimpy knees. Too high a price to pay for a few years of sport, in her opinion. She wanted him to work on his studies and someday go to college and maybe be a businessman. He could be in insurance, she said, or run a hardware store. Something respectable.

In one of the more painful ironies of his life, he ended up with a gimpy knee suffered in a far less honorable activity than football. His mother never knew.

Kohl was two years out of high school when he got in trouble and broke his mother's heart. Since then he'd been locked away in prison, his life one of misery and guilt and self-recriminations and perpetual mental visions of something dark and evil, and now he felt like an old man.

"How 'bout you?" he inquired of Danny Connor. "You got a family?"

"Wife and five kids."

Kohl made a clicking sound with his tongue but said nothing. He was in no mood to hear about Danny Connor's children, or complaints about his wife. He had no interest in problems that were not his own.

He drizzled a thin swath of catsup over the fries on his platter and ate in silence. He devoured the hamburger and onion rings and dredged the last smear of catsup from his plate with the final spike of fried potato. The food was good. Or maybe it just tasted better because this was his first meal as a free man in a very long time.

Danny Connor turned to face him, his back to the griddle.

"I suppose you know about Angie?" Danny Connor said.

"No, and I don't care to know. Whatever it is, it's nothing to me."

"Sorry. I just thought—"

"Look, if you've got something to say, spit it out and be done with it."

Danny Connor raised a hand, palm toward Kohl. "Okay. No big deal. I was going to tell you she moved out East somewhere, is all."

"Like I said, it's nothing to me."

"Well, just forget I brought it up, then."

More truckers came and went, keeping Danny Connor busy. Kohl picked up the paper bag and went to the men's room. When he'd finished there, he took a seat in a booth near the front of the dining room next to a window and opened the shade so he could see out. Ghostly white lights on tall aluminum poles lit up the parking lot.

Beyond the lighted area, a steady parade of traffic slid by on the interstate highway. He was awed by the sheer number of trucks, which formed an endless parade, one close behind the other. What would it be like to drive one of those powerful machines and haul goods from coast to coast or maybe down to Mexico? The freedom to travel hundreds or even thousands of miles over the open road should make anyone happy.

He wondered about the truck driver who had given him a ride and wished he'd learned more about the man. The truck driver didn't talk much, though, and Kohl wasn't one to ask a lot of questions.

There were cars on the highway, too, and in his mind's eye he pictured families on their way to Detroit or maybe the Upper Peninsula. It felt good to see people on the move—a gratifying view of ordinary people doing ordinary things that had been denied him for half his life.

And he wondered about Angie. For twenty years he had wanted to put her out of his mind forever and had hoped that passing time would let him forget. He had hoped in vain. Searing memories still pushed their way into his consciousness much too often, and the instant Danny Connor brought up her name his senses had come alive with the same raw images, the same sounds, the same smells, the same terror and confusion he had experienced that balmy evening two decades past.

The sky finally began to brighten on the eastern horizon. Kohl welcomed the sight. The depressing darkness soon would give way to sunshine.

Danny Connor's reflection in the windowpane warned that the fry-cook was coming toward him. Kohl was grateful for that; people slipping up from behind made him nervous. He never liked to be taken by surprise. He turned his back to the window to face the man who, so far, was his only new connection to the once-familiar world he had come back to.

"I'll be leaving in a minute," Danny Connor said. "Anything more I can do for you before the new guy and the girls come on at six o'clock?"

"I don't need anything else."

"Look, Kohl, I don't hold grudges, and as far as I'm concerned you're just as good now as anybody else that sets foot in here. You paid your price. But don't expect everybody to welcome you back with open arms. Not after what you done."

Kohl looked him in the eyes. "Yeah, well," he said, "they can take me or leave me. I'm not going to lose any sleep over it."

Danny Connor stood waiting, as if he expected Kohl to say more. After a moment of awkward silence, he turned and went back behind the counter and began scraping grease from the griddle. Kohl kept on looking out front, toward the highway. He didn't see Danny Connor leave and he didn't notice the new cook who replaced him and the two waitresses beginning their shift because they all came and went through the back door.

He had lied to Danny Connor. He hoped desperately to be accepted by the people here, the only home he'd ever known. He was not an evil person. He had not intended to do what he did. People would understand, if only he could tell the full story. All he asked was a chance to prove himself, to find a way to make a living and live out his life without being judged on his past. He did not see this as an unreasonable thing to ask.

Kohl was trying to picture Angie as she might look today when one of the waitresses approached, pad in hand and a stub of a pencil poised to write down his order. She was plain-looking and no longer young, but it felt good to have a woman close and he didn't notice her appearance. He felt guilty sitting at one of her tables with nothing in hand and, even though he really didn't want anything more, asked for coffee and a donut.

"I'll be right back with that," the waitress promised, and offered a quick smile. Maybe the smile was forced, an obligatory expression that was part of her routine to make customers feel welcome, but he didn't care. It was a sweet smile and he felt lucky she had come to take his order. Momentarily, at least, he had stopped thinking about Angie.

The waitress returned promptly and put a cup of steaming coffee on the table and then a donut, all alone on a large plate, along with silverware rolled in a paper napkin. The coffee smelled good and so did she. Her scent carried a subtle hint of something out of his past but he didn't remember what it was. Flowers his mother used to grow? Or maybe just the scent of a woman. It had been a very long time since he had experienced either. He wished he could keep this woman close.

She took his money and hurried toward the back of the room. He watched her as she walked away. Their encounter had been brief, but he felt an inexplicable sensation that here was a kindred spirit. If there was a single person in the whole world who cared to listen to his story, who possibly could understand, this waitress might be the one. He wanted her to sit across from him and talk about things she felt were important and listen as he told her how he wanted to make the most of his life now and give people reason to forget his past.

Kohl never had considered himself an optimist. But unless all the fates were working against him, he believed this would happen. Not today, maybe not anytime soon, but it would happen. He would tell this woman and she would understand. The mere fact that this was possible was in itself remarkable to him.

He took a bite of the donut and was about to sip from the cup of hot coffee when he saw the plain black Dodge sedan with a star on the door turn off the highway and charge into the parking lot. The low morning sun glinted off its windshield as it crunched to a stop in a no-parking space beside the front door. The man who got out of the car was young and overweight, dressed in a uniform that was too tight, and wore a wide leather belt around his middle that anchored a holstered handgun. He stuffed a nightstick into a loop on the belt as he walked.

The man pulled his hat on tightly as he entered the grill, looking about warily. He saw Kohl, glanced down at something in the palm of his hand, then walked directly to the booth where Kohl was seated.

"Somebody told me you were here," he said curtly. "You got business in this town, Kohl?"

"I live here."

"Not for the last twenty years, you haven't. We don't like riffraff around here. Why don't you just get on down south a ways while you're on the move and let the Indiana authorities keep track of you?"

"I'm paroled in the state of Michigan. But you know that."

The young cop slid into the booth opposite Kohl. He turned his palm upright so that Kohl could see the photograph he held, shoving it forward as if it needed to be seen up close. "Pretty good likeness," he said. "See, the fellows up at the pen send us a heads-up when scumbags like you are turned out. Complete with their latest picture. Given how good they treat you up there, I'm surprised it's not in color. This one doesn't do justice to your baby-blue eyes."

Kohl sat stoically. "You got a complaint on me or something?" he asked flatly.

"We don't need a complaint, Kohl. Look at this badge and check my nametag real close. I'm Deputy Scott Sobeski from the county sheriff's department and you're going to get to know my face good because I'll be on your ass as long as you insist on staying around here. You as much as jaywalk or spit on the sidewalk and I'll have you back behind bars in the blink of an eye. Have I made myself clear?"

"Yeah. You talk real good—for a cop."

"How long do you think you'll make it on the outside, Kohl? That smart mouth will get you in trouble real fast. People around here have long memories. You're going to catch a lot of flak, and sooner or later you'll fight back. That'll land you right back in prison. You'd come out way ahead by hanging your hat somewhere else."

"You got any more news for me, Deputy Scott Sobeski?"

"Just this bit of advice: I wouldn't be caught in the dark all by myself if I was you. Some nights it's just not safe out there."

The deputy slid from his seat and stood over Kohl, contempt in his eyes. "And one other thing," he said in a low voice, "if I was you I'd stay away from that gypsy waitress. She's got plenty of trouble of her own."

The deputy stalked out of the building and, back in his patrol car, roared out of the parking lot in a shower of dust and flying gravel. Kohl watched until the car disappeared around a corner, never changing expression. Twenty years in the state penitentiary had taught him not to show emotion. On the inside, though, he seethed with anger. He'd paid the price for what he did and no man could be more sorry nor carry a stronger sense of guilt. He remembered this town as a place with decent people who could forgive even if they couldn't forget. Had it changed that much? Or maybe he had been wrong all along.

TWO

BEYOND THE WINDOW, the day had grown bright and the sunshine sparkled on the frosted skeletons of leafless trees. Kohl finished his donut in a single bite, gulped down the rest of his coffee, retrieved the paper bag from the seat beside him, and went out. There still was a biting west wind, and he pulled his jacket tight across his chest and zipped it all the way up to where the collar began, just below his chin.

The truck stop was on the outskirts of town. From here it was no more than a half-mile to where he wanted to go. It would be an easy ten-minute walk to the old Victorian-style house where he was born and where he spent the first twenty years of his life. It was a big, two-storied house, but after Kohl's two sisters moved out West his mother had lived there alone. His sisters sent her money and paid the taxes to keep the property in the family.

He thought about his sisters as he walked. He wished he could see them—wished they would be there to welcome him home. He should be angry at them for deserting their mother, leaving her to die lonely and alone, but after years of trying to convince himself otherwise he'd finally accepted the fact that they moved away because of him, humiliated to have him as a brother after what he did. And who could blame them?

After their mother died, his sisters had turned the old house over to a company that handled cheap rentals. Kohl knew little about all this, but he'd been told by way of a brief formal letter that when the house became vacant a few months ago they had directed the company to leave it empty. He understood this, too. His sisters didn't want the place. Kohl knew they never would return. They had set things up so that he'd have a place to come back to that would keep him far away from them. And he could not blame them for this, either.

His brisk pace helped him keep warm, but with no cap and nothing to cover his face and ears the icy wind stung the patches of bare skin. *How long does it take to get serious frostbite?* He'd learned this years ago in a high school health class and he tried to recall, but too much apprehension raged through his brain and shoved aside mundane facts like how quickly exposed skin can freeze. He turned up the collar of his jacket, shifted the paper bag from one hand to the other, and thrust the free hand deep into a pocket of his trousers where he could feel the warmth of his thigh.

The sound of a vehicle coming behind him seemed out of place here, where he had felt like the only living being in an eerily silent world. He moved closer to the edge of the road. A battered old GMC pickup truck slowed to a crawl, and stopped when it came alongside. The driver was an elderly man with a weathered face and a bright red knit cap pulled down tightly on his head.

"It's a bit frosty out there this morning, lad," the driver called through an open window. "Climb in and I'll give you a ride home."

"Mr. Spencer!" Kohl recognized the voice even before he had a clear view of the face.

"Yes. And you're the Kohl boy, Ernst. Come around and get in."

Kohl would have accepted a ride from anyone who offered it just now, given the freezing cold. But he was especially grateful to see someone he knew. George Spencer lived on this road a mile beyond the Kohl house, or at any rate used to. Mr. Spencer and his father were close friends and Mr. Spencer, who had studied theology at a Lutheran seminary in Chicago but came back to the old family farm to take care of his aging mother, had given the eulogy at his father's funeral.

He hurried around the back of the truck and climbed in beside the driver. The old man extended a hand.

"It's been a long time," Kohl said. "I almost didn't recognize you. You still my closest neighbor?"

"Closest and just about the onliest now. Not many of us left out here."

"I'm glad to see you, Mr. Spencer. I'm surprised you recognized me, though."

George Spencer spoke softly. "Don't give me too much credit," he said. "I probably wouldn't have, but I knew you were coming. You were a big story on the front page of the *Gazette* last week."

"A big story? What the hell—"

"Kind of a two for the price of one deal, you might say. They wanted to let everybody know you were coming home, and it seemed like they wanted to make sure everybody knew why you'd been away."

Kohl felt a shiver run down his back. It was not from the cold, but a visceral reaction to the sudden awareness that much of his life story—the part of it he wanted to bury forever—most likely had been a topic of open discussion not only among those who knew him but also among countless strangers. Mr. Spencer's casual report should not have taken him by surprise, but it did.

"I wish they hadn't done that," was all he could think to say.

"But I suppose it's still big news, in a way," George Spencer said. He kept his voice low, almost as if the subject was one he really didn't want to discuss. "Doc Harrell was highly thought of. This is a small town. Stories like this don't come along very often around here. I doubt you would have made the papers if we lived in Detroit."

"Maybe I ought not to have come back here. I guess I could have gone to Detroit or someplace like that. Probably should have. But this is the only home I've ever had. For twenty years you dream of coming back and—"

"You did the right thing, Ernst," George Spencer interrupted. "You can still make a life for yourself here. You're still a young man, not an old-timer like me. You wouldn't have had any way to know, but Lois passed on a couple of years back."

"I'm sorry."

"She went peacefully. Said she'd had a good life. I don't find much to live for without her, though. The boys have gone to Florida and I seldom see them. The grandchildren are growing up, I suppose. But getting down there just isn't an easy trip for an old man, and it's hard for them to get up here more than a few days every year or so. I'm all alone now, and I don't feel like I have anything left to live for."

"I'm sorry, Mr. Spencer. I didn't know."

Lois Spencer had visited his mother often and always had been very nice to him and his sisters. But at this moment the grief he might have shared was overshadowed by the jolt of humiliation that struck him on hearing that he'd been front-page news. This was foolish, of course. When he had allowed himself to think about it, he had accepted the fact that his homecoming would attract attention. But that was abstract and what George Spencer had just told him was vividly concrete.

"Where are your sisters now?" the old man asked.

"Hannah's in Arizona, and I think Ada is in California, but I'm not sure."

"They both turned out to be fine young women. Your mother was very proud of them."

Kohl understood that his old friend meant no offense, and hadn't realized the inference that might be drawn from his words. But in his own mind, the mere mention of his mother's pride in his sisters was a dramatic reflection of the lack of pride she took in him. Unintentional or not, Mr. Spencer's words hurt.

As they drew close to his destination, though, Kohl's angst gave way to overflowing excitement. He really was home. He felt like a child in a fairy tale about to see the princess, almost giddy in his anticipation but at the same time nervous and uncertain.

And then he saw the house, just as the old man stopped the truck. It was nearly invisible from the road, hidden behind a wall of unpruned shrubbery and wild chokeberry and sumac. The front yard was overgrown with bluestem and switchgrass that winter frosts had left dead and stiff, adding to a general impression of dilapidation and neglect.

"Here we are, son," George Spencer said. "I hope everything's okay in there. If you want me to, I can wait 'til you check things out. You'd be welcome to come on and stay with me for a time."

"I'll make do here, Mr. Spencer. I'm not expecting too much. But I thank you for the offer."

The old man nodded and drove away. Kohl stood at the side of the road, suddenly saddened by the sight before him. From this vantage point, the old house bore little resemblance to the one he remembered. This was not the happy home of childhood memories, not the warm home where his mother and his sisters waited inside. This house was empty, cold, deserted.

But it will be home again, and I'm a free man. How could he have lost sight of this simple but immensely important truth, even for an instant? Now there was new resolve. And this would be his new anthem; he would sing it loud and clear.

He ran across the road and picked his way through the stubble to the front door. The door was locked. He would have to stop by the rental company's office and get a key. But even in this he felt modest elation. In his entire life, he never had needed a key before.

He picked his way through the weeds to the driveway that ran past the side of the house and went to the back. He could not open the back door, either, but vandals had thrown rocks through a kitchen window and knocked out most of the glass. He reached through the open space and felt with his fingers until he found a lock, released it, and hoisted the window and climbed through.

This was not the place he remembered. The silence was unnatural. His mother should be in this place, and his sisters. His homecoming would make the family complete again, and this should bring forth celebration. There should be smiles and laughter and much happy chatter.

But this was only in his memory—the way things once had been and never would be again. He could almost hear his mother's words. "Memories are like dreams," she always said. "They're only in your mind. We have to live life in the here and now." But surely she never could have imagined the future as it turned out to be.

The kitchen was cluttered with trash. Old newspapers and magazines, putrid empty food cans and milk cartons, tattered clothes and rags, cereal boxes, a bucket half-filled with paint that had dried into a solid lump entombing a small brush. The paint was an ugly mustard color and someone had started to paint the kitchen walls with it but left the work unfinished. Chunks of plaster had fallen from the ceiling.

Standing against the outer wall was a gas cooking range he believed had been his mother's, filthy with grease and the spills of things that had cooked on its surface. There was a refrigerator close to the range. Its freezer compartment door hung loosely by a single hinge. One of the overhead cabinets was missing a door and the old cast iron and enamel sink was a mass of rust.

Kohl quickly surveyed the rest of the house. First, the upstairs. Empty rooms with which he once had had what he considered an indissoluble connection. This space, so very familiar, but bare and depressing now.

Back downstairs, beyond the kitchen, there were odd bits of furniture left behind by tenants. His mother's plain oak dining table still sat in the dining room. There should be six matching chairs, but there were only three and one of these was broken, leaning haphazardly against the wall beneath a window. A dirty mattress lay on the floor of the living room, surrounded by empty beer cans and cigarette butts. A thick accumulation of old ashes packed the fireplace and rows of candle remnants in blackened jelly jars and wine bottles were arrayed across both the mantle and the hearth.

Kohl's newfound resolve melted away almost as quickly as it had come, overtaken by a new and even deeper sense of despair. This had been his home, but now it struck him as nothing more than a bleak and hopeless refuge from the swirling winds of an oncoming Michigan winter. How could it ever be home again? Home meant people, loving and caring people, and all the people were gone.

Outside, the wind had risen, and moaned gently as it swept around edges and corners of the old building. Even the natural elements mocked his folly.

It was here in this living room where the family used to gather on winter nights, sitting or lying in front of the fireplace and sharing their stories. Happy reports of the day's events, commiseration when one of them suffered disappointment or failure. He and his sisters huddled here with their mother and mourned the death of their father after an illness too short to ready them for his loss, and it was here, in this room, that a young Kohl watched with envy as his sisters, self-conscious in homemade dresses but radiant nonetheless, received their dates for high school proms and parties in town.

But on a warm spring night that was burned forever into his consciousness, all the pleasant memories were swept away like the petals of cherry blossoms in the vicious gales that often followed a late spring freeze. He stood in the exact spot where it happened. For it was in this room, too, that Kohl was arrested by sheriff's deputies who put him in handcuffs and ankle chains and took him away while his mother and sisters looked on in shock and disbelief. He imagined he could smell the smells and hear the sounds of that bleak night—sweaty bodies, lilacs blooming outside a window, thunder rumbling in the distance, his mother's choking sobs.

He flushed with shame for the hurt he'd caused his family. If only there were a way he might erase that night, make it cease to exist, purge it not just from his own brain but from the history of God's cruel world. If only he had not done that thing he did, that thing never intended, that thing brought on by the passion of a single moment—that thing too painful to be lucid in his own mind.

But hard time had taught him well. Life is stingy with second chances. A clean slate, once a mark has been etched beneath your name, will not be seen again.

Kohl grasped the mantle with both hands, leaned inward until his forehead rested against the cold wood, and wept. His sobs came silently at first, but quickly grew into loud bursts of reserved emotion. It was a long while before he pushed himself away and stood straight again, resolute, his hurt undiminished but paired now with full submission to the authenticity of his new life. And, once again, determination. In the face of ugly reality he had been rocked by despair, yes, but he was a survivor.

He retrieved the paper bag he had carried with him and dumped the contents on the bare floor so that every personal possession he owned lay before him: a razor, a comb, a toothbrush, soap and shaving cream, toothpaste, a well-used deodorant stick, two pairs of underwear, three pairs of socks, a metal cup, a spoon, a cigarette lighter, and just over five thousand dollars in cash. The money was in two thin bundles, each neatly wrapped in newspaper and tied with white cotton string. He fingered these gingerly.

His money had not come easy. Good behavior won him the privilege of a paid job in the prison's furniture and clothing factories, but at Michigan State Industries you worked hard for near-slave wages. He'd been grateful for the chance, though, and reasoned from the outset that time was on his side. One day he would be free, and a free life came with its own price. Now he worried whether he'd made enough to help pay for a fresh start.

He would need clothes. Other men in his cell block had urged him to carry an extra set of prison garb when he left confinement. It wasn't as if he would be packing a striped suit, they said. Khaki pants and shirt. That's all it would be, and he'd look like any free working man.

Now Kohl wished he had listened. But he didn't want to carry anything that wasn't essential for his very first free days and nights.

He would be a *free* man and a *free* man could buy clothes when he needed to. He had said the word with deliberate and exaggerated emphasis, good naturedly, confident that his fellow offenders would take it as he intended. They did, and his cellmate responded in kind: "Hell yeah. That's a *free* man's privilege. But don't blame us if you piss your pants and don't have a dry pair to put on."

Memories again. Positive memories among so many ugly ones, recollections of men he had become close to, sharing as they did the universal experiences of those locked behind bars. These were men he likely never would have found much in common with under different circumstances. But whatever tough front they put up, whatever crime they had committed, there was within each of them a streak of human caring and compassion. They had been sincere in wishing him well in the outside world some of them might never know again.

For now, though, his immediate concern was not clothes, but heat. He gathered some of the old newspapers from the kitchen, crumpled them and put them in the fireplace and looked around for something to burn. A broken child's highchair lay in a corner. He lifted it high and smashed it against the floor. It shattered into a dozen pieces, which he laid on the newspaper. He ignited the paper with his lighter and the dry wood caught fire quickly. After a few moments he could feel the heat bleeding out into the room.

Once he was sure the fire was burning well, he retrieved the cash he'd carried in his paper bag and took it upstairs. Inside a closet, the secret hiding place he had counted as secure since he was a teenager was just the same as it always had been. It took only seconds to find the loose plank in the floor. He lifted it and placed the bills in the space beneath, then carefully replaced the plank.

He went back to the kitchen and to the back door, which he thought was locked. It had no lock, but the door was warped and stuck. He gave it a forceful jerk and it opened. An icy wind blew from the southwest, whipping up such dead leaves as weren't frozen to the ground and raising them in swirls like little tornadoes as they were driven against the house. Kohl shielded his face with his hands.

This old house once had been the center of life on his grandfather's farm. His father inherited it, but soon gave up farming and sold the land. The family kept the house and outbuildings and the acre of ground they sat on. The barn had long since been torn down and carted away, board by board, and the only outbuilding that remained was a small shed that at one time had served as a smokehouse for curing meat. It was weather-beaten and leaning and looked as though it would collapse with the next gust of wind.

But he was happy to find that the livestock water well, its ancient iron pump intact, quickly produced a forceful stream. Kohl felt a small surge of elation. Whatever he might lack, he had an abundant supply of clean water. Surely this balanced the scales a bit on the positive side!

A modest remnant of the farm's woodlot was overgrown with briars and brushy undergrowth, but a few aging white and red oaks, a solitary black gum tree, and a thicket of honey locusts still offered firewood. He picked up fallen branches under two of the oaks, all he could carry, and lugged them into the house, stumbling over the threshold and barely escaping a hard fall. He hoped he had enough fuel to keep the fireplace burning for at least a few hours.

If he could find a container to fill with water at the pump and later walk back to town and bring home some food, his most critical short-term needs would be taken care of. For now, he would have the means to keep himself alive.

But first things first. That's what his mother always said. He remembered her gentle voice, "Now, kids, first things first."

He spent the next hour making the house more habitable, clearing piles of rubbish from the kitchen and building a temporary trash heap just outside the back door. He stacked the newspapers and magazines in a corner and sorted the old clothes and rags, carrying those clean enough to use into the living room and tossing them on the floor near the mattress. He saved everything he thought might be burned in the fireplace.

When he'd done all he could, he sat on the cold floor in the living room and leaned back against a wall. The nagging ache in his leg had grown more intense.

It was hard to believe he really was a free man. The change had been too sudden. Only hours ago he'd awakened in his cramped cell after a near sleepless night, afraid that his pending release was a dream, that he still had years to serve and freedom would remain a painful illusion. Even as he went through final processing he'd been scared that something would go wrong. Was there something that could turn up in his record and lead them to renege on his promised liberty and keep him locked up? He desperately hoped there was not.

He was silent in the prison van that took him and two others to the bus station, too nervous to speak of freedom. And when he learned that he'd have to wait another day before there was a bus for home he nearly panicked. If he waited around the bus station he might be mistaken for someone else, a wanted criminal. Or arrested for vagrancy. Or robbed of the money that was his last best hope. And so he walked to the edge of town and thumbed a ride, naively unaware that hitchhiking on the interstate highway might be illegal and grateful to the tractor-trailer driver who stopped, who welcomed him to a seat in the high cab of the massive Kenworth, no questions asked.

But he was home. He was free and he was set to begin life over, a great and wonderful truth that finally was beginning to sink in. He would face whatever lay in store with all the strength he could muster, and at some point this all would seem natural. Just now, though, he felt very much alone.

THREE

IT STILL WAS dark when Kohl woke in the morning. The room was freezing cold. Sometime in the middle of the night he had roused himself by his own restlessness and lay awake for several minutes listening for the familiar prison noises. When his brain unfogged he knew where he was and quickly went to sleep again, but his mind was not at ease. Dreams took him back to guarded cells and lockdowns intermingled with unclear visions of Angie in settings that had no relevancy.

He was determined to make the best of this day, and all the days to come. One day at a time. This was the way he had survived twenty years in prison, and he had vowed to approach life as a free man the same way. He would make gains on some front—even though they might be modest—each and every day.

Kohl was not particularly religious. He had gone to church with Angie, but for him these were social occasions. He never had taken a sermon seriously, and the only real discussion about God he'd ever been a part of was with a prison chaplain. Nothing personal. He and a dozen others from his cellblock in a mandatory "morals" session the warden had thought up as a way to impress some committee of state legislators.

Most of what the chaplain said that day went in one ear and out the other, but one thing had stuck with him. "God is neutral. He's neither for you nor against you," the chaplain proclaimed. "And keep in mind, He has lots of ground to cover. If you want God's attention, you have to make that first contact." The neutrality part contradicted what little he recalled from sermons in Angie's church, but the idea of making first contact seemed to him to make a good deal of sense.

He had seen prisoners turn to God and change their ways, and he had seen prisoners pretend to turn to God in an effort to polish up applications to the parole board. He had yet to see anything resembling a miracle. And how would God have time for an insignificant mortal like him, anyway? Like the prison chaplain said, God surely must have a lot to do.

"God, I could use your help," Kohl said aloud. "The chaplain said I'd have to make the first contact. I guess this is it." Feeling a bit foolish, he looked about, as if expecting someone else to be in the room to hear. With or without God, he thought to himself, he had to get out and get something to eat. *And, God, if you happen to be watching I wouldn't mind somebody having my back.*

He made a quick list of things he needed most, zipped two fifty-dollar bills securely in a jacket pocket, and set out for town. The sun was barely visible above the eastern horizon as he went out through the back door and made his way around the house to the road. A bitterly cold wind blew off Lake Michigan miles to the west.

Kohl walked at a pace as brisk as he could manage on his bad leg, and sooner than expected he could see Swearington's Market in the distance. This is where he would buy his own groceries for the first time in his life. Not such a big deal, maybe, but his mood was buoyed. He could feel his heart beat faster in his eagerness to take this modest first step toward living a normal existence.

There should be a half-dozen vehicles in the Swearington's parking lot on a crisp winter morning like this, but as he walked closer he could see that the lot was empty. And then he saw why. Swearington's Market no longer existed. What he recalled as a busy little store was nothing more than an empty shell of a building squatting gauntly amidst the weeds. The asphalt surface of the parking lot was faded to an anemic gray, its once vivid yellow striping all but invisible.

Kohl had given no thought to the likelihood of changes in the landscape he remembered. He had no backup plan. But he had to have food, and there really was no choice except to find another place to buy what he needed. He kept on walking, still on the outskirts of town where there was no sidewalk. A dimly visible footpath marked his way along the shoulder of the road, where the irregular frozen ground and clumps of dead weeds and grass made for hard walking. He stumbled once and nearly fell. The misstep sent a sharp pain up the leg to his bad knee and he was forced to slow his pace.

Conditions improved at the city limits, with a sidewalk on one side of the street. He had been walking for twenty minutes when he first caught sight of a combination grocery store and pharmacy a half-block ahead. He forced himself to walk faster in spite of the pain in his knee and was warm from exertion when he got to the little store and went inside. The store was hot, especially on the east side where sunlight streamed in through two high windows, and the heat and an array of odors he couldn't identify made the air stifling.

As Kohl made his way through the narrow aisles that ran between well-stocked shelves, his image was constantly reflected in a large parabolic mirror mounted on the back wall so that he was visible to anyone up front. He got cheap staples—beans, rice, and pasta—and a box of plain vanilla wafers, then added two cans each of corn, peas, and tomatoes to his shopping basket. The feeling that he was under surveillance gave him a strong urge to finish quickly and get out of this place.

A slovenly woman who looked to be about his age stood behind the checkout counter chewing on a finger nail. She eyed him coldly as he approached.

"I read they were letting you out," she said.

The woman did not look familiar and Kohl doubted she'd ever known him. "I beg your pardon," he said softly.

"I said, I read they were letting you out. I didn't expect to see you in here, though."

"Ma'am, I just want to pay for my groceries and be on my way."

This was not true.

He wanted to confront this woman. Who was she and how did she know him? He wanted to stand there and look her in the eye and fight back. He wanted to say that he was a free man, that he'd served his time and paid his price. He wanted to tell her there was a side to the story that she didn't know, that he was not evil and never intended for that dreadful thing to happen.

The woman glared at him. "Oh, I'll take your money," she said. "And then I'd like you to be on your way, all right. And don't come back. People around here haven't forgot you, and they won't likely forget what you did. It don't matter how long it's been."

Kohl gave her one of his fifty-dollar bills and got back just over thirty dollars in change. The woman shoved his money across the counter rudely. She said nothing more and he took his money and the things she had thrown together in three plastic bags and walked out. His quick shopping experience had given him new perspective. Winning back his good name might be more difficult than he'd hoped, and prices had gone up much more than he realized. His money wouldn't last long.

But this woman would not bring him down. He owed her nothing. What likelihood was there that he'd ever see her again, given that he would never return to her store? He had food now, and the old house would give him shelter. His reintegration into society might be rocky, but he was a free man and he would do whatever it took to gain acceptance. And he would be patient. As he had come to understand in prison, the passing of time could no more be rushed than it could be slowed.

Kohl wanted to see Danny Connor. The ugly reception he had just received at the market magnified the charity of Danny's welcome the night before. Danny could be a friend and just now friends were in short supply. And anyway, although it had taken a while for him to realize this, he liked Danny Connor.

He thought about the waitress. Unless she was off today she would be there now. It was an easy rationalization. A cheap breakfast with good coffee was very appealing, he could get this at the Purple Onion Grill, and the Purple Onion Grill was not far away. He started walking in that direction with a good deal more enthusiasm than he'd had when he left home on this frigid morning.

Danny Connor wasn't there. "He's been gone a couple of hours now," the fry-cook on duty reported. "Can't anybody else help you?"

Kohl told him no and walked back to the front of the dining room. His arms were tired from carrying the groceries and he needed to put the bags down. He set them on the table of the same booth he'd occupied before, next to a front window, and slid onto the green vinyl-covered bench. His knees were stiff and his feet hurt.

He hadn't seen her when he came in and he felt a surge of pleasure when he saw her approaching.

"Well, good morning," she said. Her face was animated and her eyes reinforced her smile. "I didn't expect to see you back so soon. Late breakfast or early lunch?"

Kohl wanted to appear dispassionate. Just another patron looking for hot food and strong coffee and respite from the cold. He wanted his response to sound casual, detached. "Whatever," he told her. "I'm hungry. You got a special or anything?"

"Let me get you some meatloaf. It comes with mashed potatoes and fresh-baked bread. You want gravy?"

"Yes, please."

"And you'll want coffee?"

"Sure. Anything hot."

Kohl watched as she went toward the back, making out an order as she walked. Surely the intense attraction he felt toward this woman was silly. He was forty-one years old, behaving like a love-sick school boy who'd just noticed that his first-grade teacher was prettier than his mother. Hadn't he matured enough to know better? Or did he have to act like a teenager again, hoping somehow to make up the years he'd missed? He wanted not to embarrass himself.

She soon had food on his table—a large square of meatloaf with a mound of mashed potatoes smothered in brown gravy at its side. She also brought a small basket that held a miniature loaf of bread. And a whole pot of coffee.

"Let me know if you need anything else," she said, and rushed away to another customer.

It wasn't likely that any of the others seated in the grill's small dining area or on stools at the counter in the back would know who he was, Kohl reasoned. Most looked to be truck drivers, and the parking lot was filled with big over-the-road rigs similar to the one he'd ridden in on only hours earlier. He had seen none of these drivers before and they hadn't seen him, and it seemed unlikely that his newest nemesis, Deputy Scott Sobeski, would be back again this soon. Sobeski no doubt was going to be a very sharp thorn in his side, but for now he could eat his food and drink his coffee in peace, and not worry that he was being stared at from behind.

He would be rested when he finished. He would speak to her again and she would invite him to come back and he'd go home and begin to make the old house more habitable. After his rough outing in town, he found consolation in the thought of staying inside for the rest of the day and getting his home in order. *His* home. The home of a free man. And yet he was reluctant to leave the comfort of the grill. There were other people here. Free people, like him, who could come and go as they pleased—stay all day if they wanted to, or leave right now.

It wasn't so much that Kohl was interested in these people as individuals and he had no interest in striking up friendships. But these were ordinary people, living life the way it should be lived. And he was one of them. He was an ordinary person, not a prisoner. He reveled anew in this remarkable sensation.

The waitress returned and poured a fresh cup of coffee. She asked if he would like anything more. Kohl said no, he really needed to get moving.

"It's cold out there, hon," the waitress said. "May as well stay for a while."

"Yes, I'd like to. But I got too much to do."

"You work someplace close?"

"No. I have a lot of work to do on my house."

He yearned for her to say more. He would respond, and for this brief moment in time they would be talking, face-to-face. She took his money and thanked him and encouraged him to stop in again, and although he knew there was nothing personal in her words he sensed that they were genuine. She was genuine. He had seen enough phonies in his life to know the difference.

Kohl zipped his jacket and turned up the collar so that he could feel it against the back of his neck, picked up his bags of groceries and went back out into the cold. His mind raced with all the new things he had to think about. He hadn't enough money, and people were not going to accept him back and forgive him for what he'd done. Not easily. The woman in the market probably was typical of what he could expect. He could only hope there also might be others like Danny Connor.

But most of all he thought about the waitress. He could not forget the smell of her, the softness of her voice, the way she accepted him as an ordinary working man. He wished he'd stayed longer at the Purple Onion.

He set out for home, this time walking into the wind. The gusts seemed even stronger than when he left the house at sunrise. Icy pellets beat against his bare skin. He stopped and put down the bags of groceries so that he could use his hands to warm his face and ears. He rubbed the exposed areas of skin vigorously until the cold was gone and circulation was restored.

He pushed ahead with all the effort he could muster. Damned bad knee! If he had two good legs he could walk faster. The cold was good incentive, but his level of anger and frustration also played a heavy role. Pleasing mental images of the waitress were pushed aside by the spiteful words of the grocery store clerk. *"People around here haven't forgot you, and they won't likely forget what you did. It don't matter how long it's been."* He finished the walk home at a punishing pace.

It was almost as cold inside the old house as it was outdoors. He piled wood in the fireplace, kindled it with old newspapers, and soon had a warm fire. He unpacked his grocery bags and placed things carefully in the rickety kitchen cabinets, braced himself to face the bitter cold again, and started out to get more wood for the fireplace. He was about to open the door when a sound from outside caused him to stop short. A whine. A cry for help, pleading and pitiful.

He opened the door carefully. A small black and white dog, shivering from the cold—or maybe from fear—stared up at him through eyes filled with hope. The animal was emaciated and dirty, its long coat matted and thick with burrs.

"Good lord!" Kohl exclaimed. "You need help, dog. Let's get you in here and see what I can do."

He pushed the door open wider with his foot and lifted the trembling animal from the frozen ground, carried it to the living room, and put it down in front of the fire. The dog offered neither gratitude nor resistance. It merely cowered at his feet, looking up with an empty stare as if ready to surrender itself completely and accept whatever lay in store.

"Looks like you've had it pretty rough, little guy," Kohl said. "I'd say you may need a friend even more than I do. And that's saying a lot, okay?"

He left the dog and went to the kitchen and found a battered aluminum sauce pan, took it outside to the well and rinsed it under the pump, then filled it with fresh water. When he got back inside the dog was asleep. He placed the pan of water on the floor near the dog's nose and piled more wood on the fire. The room was warm. Kohl was grateful for the old house's thick brick walls that compensated for the drafty doors and windows.

He needed to use the toilet and the only way he could do that was to bring in more water. He would have to fill the tank so that the toilet could be flushed. One flush at a time and refill before each use.

This might not be the most convenient way to make the old house's plumbing work, but for now it was the only way he had.

He had to carry in two pans of water to fill the tank high enough to flush. This meant that, until he got a pail that held a lot more water than the sauce pan, he'd find himself making far too many trips between the house and the pump out back. A large water pail moved to the top of his growing wish list.

When Kohl finished upstairs, he found the dog still sleeping in front of the fireplace and felt a mild sense of relief. What? Had he been afraid the animal might be gone? Was he this much attached to the dog already? He did not need a dog to care for, another mouth to feed, another living thing to protect and shelter.

But as he looked down on the sleeping dog, his doubts quickly melted away. This was something good. This animal asleep before him was not human, but it offered companionship. He was no longer alone.

"You're a survivor," he said softly, stroking the dog's head. "We're both survivors. Maybe it was meant for us to get together out here. It's me and you against the world, pup. And, hey, against a team like us the world had better watch out! You hear what I'm saying? "

At the sound of Kohl's voice, the dog stirred, repositioning its head from one extended front leg to the other. Kohl kept on stroking, his hand moving gingerly down the back of the dog's neck and along its spine. He could feel the bones, jagged under the thin layer of flesh and the coat of thick long hair. This animal soon would have died of starvation even if not from the cold.

"I think you got here just in time," he said. "I don't have any dog food, but I'll find something for you to eat."

The uncooked beans and rice and pasta he had just unpacked were out of the question. That left the cookies. Kohl opened the box and shook a half-dozen or so of the wafers into his hand. He took these back to the dog and held them close in front of its nose. The dog roused quickly, sniffed the cookies and then gulped them down in a single swallow. It was wide awake in an instant. It rose to a standing position, alert and eager. Kohl was grateful to see it animated and lively, like a different creature from the one that had come whimpering to his back door.

"You need these more than I do," he said. "I'll get you the rest of them."

The dog ate all the cookies, then lapped up a long drink from the pan of water. Minutes later, it was asleep again in front of the fire.

Kohl sat beside it like a worried mother. Occasionally he reached down and stroked the animal's head, touching gently so as not to wake it. He wanted to comb the burrs from its coat but surely that could wait until it had slept and rested.

FOUR

HE DID NOT remember lying down, but sometime in the afternoon, stretched out on the hard floor next to the dog, Kohl woke from a sound sleep. Stiff joints told him he'd slept for some time. He was immediately wide awake and alert, a survival reflex gained from years of sleeping in dangerous surroundings and a signal that something external had caused him to wake suddenly. It was not the dog, which lay silently, still asleep, apparently not having moved so much as an inch in any direction.

The wind blowing through the branches of the oak trees behind the house made an eerie, almost mournful sound. The fire was nearly out and the room was cold. Kohl pulled himself up to a sitting position and looked toward the kitchen, where he'd been stacking the firewood. There was none. He remembered that he'd been on his way to get more when he found the dog at his door.

"Damn," he muttered, straining to lift himself to a standing position. "What now?"

He got a quick answer. Someone was at the front door, beating forcefully, as if facing an emergency and frantic to get attention. Kohl rushed to the door and called through it, "I'm here. Come to the back."

"Open the damn door, Kohl."

"It's stuck, and hard to open. Who's out there?"

"Deputy Sobeski. I want to talk to you. Open the door. Now. Or do you want me to kick it in?"

Kohl cursed under his breath. He grasped the doorknob and turned it, then pulled hard. The door was warped and swollen from weeks of bad weather with no interior heat to dry it out. It held tight. Sobeski kicked hard at the bottom edge and broke it loose and Kohl pulled it open.

"You'd have busted in, wouldn't you?" he demanded.

"Damn right I would. I'm on police business here, Kohl."

"You could have gone around back."

"I'm not about to get my boots muddy just to satisfy a felon like you."

"I served my time, Sobeski. You know that."

"Once a con always a con. You're not going to make it on the outside, Kohl. You'll be back behind the walls before the winter's out. I've seen enough of your kind to know."

"You said police business. Let's get to it."

Sobeski pushed further into the room and looked about. The dog, awakened by the commotion, slunk toward the two men, eyeing the deputy nervously. Kohl reached out to it and laid a hand on its back.

"I see you got yourself a dog," Sobeski said. "Had it vaccinated and all that stuff? I don't see a collar. It's illegal to let a dog run around loose in this county, so it looks like I'm going to have to write you a ticket. You got two-hundred dollars to pay a ticket, Kohl?"

"Damn it, Sobeski, that's not my dog. It's a stray that showed up at my door a while ago. I let it in and fed it and let it get warm. Want to write me a ticket? Go ahead. I'd be glad to stand in front of a judge on it. You'd come out looking like a fool."

Sobeski stiffened. "It'll be a cold day in hell when you make me look like a fool," he said. "But that's not what I came out here for, anyway. I'll be back another day to check on your dog. Right now I need to take a good look around this place. You're on parole. You wouldn't have any weapons stashed away somewhere, would you?"

"You got a warrant?"

"Seems to me like you invited me in. If I need a warrant I can get one in thirty minutes, and then I'll be back and tear this place apart. Or you can be polite and ask me to look around now."

Kohl was determined not to let his anger show. He stepped aside, extending an arm. "Be my guest," he said, careful not to sound sarcastic.

Sobeski tromped past him into the kitchen. He looked about the room hurriedly, then returned to where Kohl stood. The dog lay at

Kohl's feet. The deputy stepped close to the fireplace and made a show of leaning in and looking up as if inspecting the chimney.

"Be careful you don't get burned," Kohl said, this time making no effort to hide his mockery.

"Never know what a shithead like you might have hid up there," the deputy responded. "This place got an upstairs?"

"The stairs are right there."

Sobeski disappeared up the stairway, his boots clomping on the wood steps. Kohl heard him walk about in the upstairs bedrooms. "Wish the sonofabitch would fall through the floor," he said, speaking low-voiced to the dog. The dog looked up as if it understood.

After only a few minutes, the deputy was back. "Real upscale place you got here," he said. "I wonder if the housing authority ought not to get out and inspect it, seeing as how you don't have a flush toilet and who knows how many other code violations. I think I might get in touch with 'em tomorrow." He brushed by Kohl and the dog, then paused at the door and looked back. "You'll be seeing a lot of me, Kohl," he said. "Get used to it!"

Deputy Sobeski went out the same way he'd entered. He left the door standing open. A blast of cold air reminded Kohl that he had to get more firewood.

He soon had a stack of dead oak branches in the kitchen, enough, he hoped, to last through the night. He carried four of the smaller ones to the fireplace and laid them, one branch at a time, on the hot ashes. When the fire didn't catch immediately, he used some of the newspaper as kindling. The paper flared brightly, flames licking at the dry wood, and soon the fire was burning fiercely and radiating heat into the room again.

The dog woke, limped to Kohl and lay down at his feet. When he looked into its eyes, Kohl was moved to an even deeper level of sympathy. This friendless animal was vulnerable to every danger in the world. It had put its trust in him and needed his help if it was to survive.

"I'll take care of you," he said softly. "From now on, we're in this together."

Both the man and the dog were wide awake now. Thanks to his unplanned nap during the afternoon, Kohl felt as though he'd had plenty of sleep. He was hungry and he knew the dog was still in dire need of food. He pulled on his shoes and his jacket, picked up the sauce pan the dog had drunk from, and went out through the kitchen door into the cold outdoor world beyond.

The iron handle of the pump was like ice and he was reminded that he must get gloves as soon as possible. And a warm coat and cap. He couldn't make it for long without them, and now he had another reason to keep himself alive.

Back inside, he set the pan of water in the edge of the fire. When the water began to boil he filled the pan with shell pasta from one of the boxes he'd picked up at the market. He hadn't found a can opener among the surviving kitchen utensils, but there was a butcher knife and a stubby paring knife in one of the drawers, and he used the butcher knife to cut open the top of a can of beans. He put the can on the hearth, near the open blaze.

When the pasta had cooked long enough, he raked the pan out of the fire and, using old magazine pages to insulate his hands against burns, took it to the kitchen sink. He drained the pasta as best he could and fanned it with the sheets of paper to hurry cooling. Once it was no longer hot to his touch, he took the pan back to the living room and set it before the dog. The animal wolfed down the pasta in a few gulps, licked the pan clean, and looked up expectantly.

Kohl had managed only a few quick bites of the warm beans. He was still hungry, which made him even more sympathetic to the dog.

"Sorry, buddy," he said. "That's all there is for now. Don't think you'd go for my beans. But I'll get out as soon as it's daylight and get you some real food—you know, the good stuff, made for dogs and not humans. But I guess the pasta tasted pretty good, eh?"

If the dog hoped for more, it made no protest. It lay down at his feet, front paws extended and chin on its forelegs, its tail wrapped carefully around the hind quarters closest to the fire. Kohl stooped and ran a hand over the dog's back. The fur was dirty and matted, thin in spots so that he could see patches of rough and reddened skin. He would need to get something to treat it with.

The dog was asleep again. Kohl watched the rhythmic rise and fall of its belly that marked the animal's easy breathing and considered the helplessness and the pain and the terror he'd seen in its eyes only hours before. Now it was warm and had food and water and was very much at rest.

"As long as I eat, you'll eat," he said, dropping to his knees beside the tranquil animal. "If I can manage to get by, myself, you won't have anything to worry about. I'll do whatever it takes. Like I said before, it's you and me against the world. You're going to be family."

He lay beside the dog and put his arm across it and the dog took in a long, deep breath and let it out slowly—a sigh of contentment that made Kohl feel like a million dollars. It had taken so little to make this innocent creature feel secure.

"When we get you healthy again you'll be tough as nails," he whispered, speaking close to the dog's ear. "You need a tough name. I'm going to call you Jake. And people better understand that you and me go together, Jake. Some joker steps on your tail, I chop off his foot! Somebody's got a problem with you, they come to me. Somebody gives me a hard time, you bite 'em on the hairy ass. What do you think about that, Jake? We got a deal?"

Jake had begun to snore. Kohl laughed.

Daylight would not come for several hours, and even when it did he would be in no hurry to go out into the cold again. He lay beside the dog, alert, his mind rushing from one thing to another. A litany of things he needed to do demanded attention but slipped away. His life story intruded in small flashes. Angie, trivial worries, the minutiae of human experience all weighed on his consciousness as never before.

He thought about his mother. Surely he would have been let out of prison long enough to come home for her funeral if there was a merciful god watching over the universe. They could have brought him in chains if they had to. But the system wasn't set up for that, they said, and obviously mercy for him was the lowest priority for anyone at the penitentiary who had an ounce of authority.

He wondered about some of the men still in prison, especially three who had become close friends. Two would be catching the chain pretty soon—getting out on parole if they didn't screw up— but a man named David Murray McKenzie, a former hockey player whom Kohl had found to be a very decent human being, was serving a life sentence with no chance of being released. "Only the back door parole for me, and I'm good with that," he told Kohl early on. He apparently had reconciled himself to dying in prison. But earthly surroundings didn't matter, he said, because he had put himself in God's hands.

His thoughts returned time and again to Angie, their carefree days, teenaged friends falling in love. But when did love begin? They wanted to be together, even as children. He remembered a summer day when Angie, maybe ten or eleven years old, persuaded an older friend to walk all the way to the country to visit Kohl's sisters. Her ulterior motive was to come along to see him. Before the day was over, her crafty plan caused something of a panic when her mother found her missing.

He had known so little about girls, and had acted on the basis of assumptions that he knew now were wrong. In his blind devotion then, he couldn't imagine doing the things with her that other boys claimed to have done with other girls. His rigid confidence that Angie would be offended if he tried those things with her had proved bitterly ironic.

And he thought about the waitress. He wanted to see her and hear her voice. He wanted to talk with her and hear her stories. He wanted to know her, let her know him.

She would hear the things other people said soon enough and understand why he was loathed and shunned. Like Danny Connor, she might be willing to give him another chance. But Kohl wouldn't take that gamble. He vowed to tell her the whole story, from the beginning, the full story that no one ever had heard—not even his mother and sisters nor the lawyer who defended him—and she would recognize the truth and know that it was not malevolence that led him to do what he did.

Kohl pulled the old mattress as close to the fireplace as he dared, barely disturbing the sleeping dog. He lay down beside the animal again and pulled a layer of old newspapers over him like a blanket. He gently pulled the dog close against him. The night was still, except for the sounds of Michigan winter. Timbers in the old house creaked as they shrank with the bitter cold, even though they'd been through a hundred changing seasons. Outside, the wind came in short gusts, blowing icy snow pellets against the windows. He was glad to have shelter, here in his own house, and he was grateful to have a companion. At this moment he felt as close to Jake as he ever had felt to another living being.

As the night wore on, Kohl finally slept. But he was up again as soon as the faint light of dawn began to filter into the room. He tried to bend and stretch the aches from his back and knees, rousing Jake in the process. Jake went to the kitchen door and barked and waited expectantly, but patiently, until Kohl came to his aid.

"I'll turn you out if you promise not to run away," Kohl said.

"And when you get back inside we'll make some more pasta. Sorry we don't have any of the good stuff yet."

He pulled open the door and the dog hesitated for an instant, then ran out. Kohl picked up more firewood under the oak trees and stacked it in the kitchen and took the sauce pan to the well and pumped it full of water. Back inside, he stirred the coals in the fireplace and, after breaking them into shorter pieces over his knee, judiciously placed two of the smaller oak branches on the budding flame. He had the pan of pasta boiling at the edge of the fire when Jake scratched at the door.

The dog appeared to understand that food was on the way. Kohl got the pasta ready as fast as he could. Jake gobbled it down.

"Sorry, fellow, that's all there is for now," Kohl said. "But I'll be going out in a bit, and when I come back you'll have all you can eat. I promise."

Jake wagged his tail, the first time he had done so since coming into the house. He watched Kohl intently. His ears stood up when Kohl spoke.

"You may be the toughest dog in Michigan, Jake. And smart! And you're my buddy. That makes me a lucky man."

Jake lay down near the fireplace and went back to sleep. Kohl brought in another pan of water and heated it, shaved, and washed up as best he could. His clothes were dirty and wrinkled. More clothes and a place to do laundry were added to his list of things he needed. The list was getting long. For now, though, his immediate goal was to get to the Baum Farm Supply store, where his mother used to go for rat poison, and buy medicine for Jake's skin sores. He could get dog food there, too, and probably some of the other things he needed.

He hoped the Baum Farm Supply store was still there.

FIVE

IT WAS TWO hours after sunrise and bitter cold when Kohl set out for town. He felt good, not because of the brisk walk in the frigid air, but because he had new purpose. He had been concerned only for himself, but now he had Jake to take care of. He was needed.

The farm supply store still stood on the busy corner where it always had been, hardly changed from the way he remembered except that it appeared to be somewhat run down. There was no one in the store who looked familiar and no one seemed to know who he was, and he felt at ease moving about the musty-smelling array of merchandise and pretending interest in things he knew nothing about.

A young woman named Amy, who looked no older than fifteen or sixteen, helped him find medicated salve for Jake's sores. She assured him it was very effective; she had used it on her own dog and it worked well. He became somewhat flustered when she asked what kind of dog Jake was and he had to admit he didn't know. He didn't want to tell her that Jake had just come into his life and he knew nothing of his past.

"Well, you can't beat a good old mixed breed," Amy said. "I like to think they have the best qualities of everything in the mix. Myself, I don't want a purebred anything. Not that I could afford one if I did."

"Yeah, well. Anyway, somebody needs to take care of the regular kind."

"I don't mean to be nosey, but I don't remember seeing you around. Are you a local?"

"I live out on Old Church Road."

"Oh, yeah," Amy said, her expression indicating sudden awareness. "I know where that is. That old empty farm house out there's where some of the kids get together every once in a while and party. Just between us, I think they do drugs. But that's a gang I don't have any part of."

"Good for you. And thanks very much for your help."

"Hey, no problem. You take care of that dog."

He looked around the store another ten minutes or so and saw any number of things he wished he could buy. He stuck to his prepared list, though, and went to the checkout counter with an axe, a five-gallon plastic pail, a ten-pound bag of dry dog food, matches, and a simple, inexpensive can opener. The middle-aged man behind the counter greeted him pleasantly and thanked him for his business. Amy waved goodbye from the back of the store as he left.

He left Baum much more hopeful that gaining acceptance might be possible, after all. A few instances of friendly treatment such as he had just experienced would balance the painful ones. But there still was no escape from the nervous uncertainty he could count on any time he went to some place new.

Eager as he was to get the food home to Jake, the temptation to go by the Purple Onion was more than he could resist. Once again, the easy rationale. It was not far out of his way and he needed breakfast. He had to take care of himself if he were to care for his dog. And anyway, Jake probably was sound asleep and wouldn't miss him for another couple of hours.

She was there.

She looked up just as he first saw her, and although he quickly turned his head it was too late. She could not have missed his wistful gaze, nor his flush of self-consciousness when their eyes met. For an instant he considered bolting out the door and rushing away, but common sense overtook him just in time. Such a move would put an even finer point on his foolish behavior.

He took a seat in the booth he had sat in before, in the front of the grill's dining area near a window. He'd barely settled into it by the time she reached his table.

"Welcome back," she said, and Kohl thought her smile was beautiful.

"Hi."

"You must be new in town. Since I hadn't seen you around until the other day, I thought maybe you were just passing through."

"I've been away," Kohl told her. "But I live here."

Ordering breakfast was a formality to which he gave little consideration. She could have brought him whatever she chose. He said coffee and bacon and eggs without looking at the menu she put before him, leaning in close, and he felt his own heartbeat pounding in his temples in response to her nearness. He watched her walk away, but saw neither her plumpness nor the ruddy, feathery veins in the calves of her bare legs. He didn't notice the swelling in her ankles from having a job that kept her on her feet all day. What he saw was a beautiful woman with elegance in every movement.

She went to the counter at the back of the grill and gave her order to the fry-cook, who looked up and appeared to be saying something serious. She listened until he finished talking, then turned back toward Kohl and was beside him again in an instant.

"They tell me you're Kohl," she said, standing at the end of his table and pouring coffee from a darkly stained carafe.

"Yes. And it says on the nametag that your name is Cara."

"Yeah, it is. But they wouldn't let me spell it the way I really do. They thought it was too hard or something."

"How else could you spell 'Cara'?"

"It's Irish. It's spelled C-a-r-a-g-h. It means 'friend'—at least that's what I've been told."

"Friend. I like that. Nobody needs a friend more than I do, Cara."

"Don't push your luck."

"I never push my luck. Never had any to push."

Cara laughed. "Sounds like we've got something in common," she said.

"Can I ask you a question?"

"Sure. Go ahead."

"How come Sobeski called you a gypsy if you're Irish?"

"Because I'm an Irish Traveler. That dumb ass wouldn't know the difference."

"I guess I'm as dumb as he is. What's an Irish Traveler?"

Cara glanced quickly over her shoulder, toward the back of the dining room, and slipped into the seat opposite Kohl. "We're not doing much business this morning," she said. "I may as well sit a while. I mean, do you mind?"

"Oh, no," Kohl said quickly. "I'm glad for your company."

"Okay. So you were asking what's an Irish Traveler."

"Yes. If that's what you are."

"Yep, that's what I am." She was looking Kohl straight in the eyes. "Lots of people think we're gypsies. You and Sobeski are not the only ones who don't know the difference."

"But I thought gypsies were dark-skinned people. You've got red hair and green eyes."

"Romany gypsies are, for the most part. I think they started out in India or someplace. We're different folks completely. Just think of us as the original Irish. Your bacon and eggs should be ready. I'll be right back."

Cara slid from behind the table and walked toward the back of the room. Kohl took a long drink of hot coffee. The fact that she had just been there, talking with him as if they were friends, made him want her presence even more. He turned and looked just in time to see the fry-cook shove a serving platter across the counter and Cara pick it up, balance it on the flat of her hand and hoist it shoulder high. She brought a plate of scrambled eggs and bacon and a stack of blackened toast.

"This ought to hold you for a while," she said, and to Kohl's surprise she slid back into the seat across the table.

Kohl didn't know what to say. He fumbled with his fork, stabbed at the eggs, and finally picked up a strip of bacon with his fingers. When he looked up, Cara was watching him like a worried mother concerned about an inept child.

"I seen all that stuff you're carrying," she said. "You need transportation, Kohl."

Kohl started to answer through a mouthful of food, but caught himself. He held up a hand while he finished chewing. He swallowed hard, wiped his mouth with a napkin, and said, "I just moved and I've not had time to think about a car yet. I can walk for now—until the really bad weather sets in, anyway."

"But packing all that stuff?" She motioned toward the axe he had stood against the wall and the pail, sitting on the floor at the end of his seat and holding the dog food and the smaller items. "That's going to get pretty heavy."

"Yeah, well. I can always put it down and rest a minute."

"Look," Cara said, "I just asked Jack if I could leave early and take the rest of the day off. I've got time coming. And this place ain't going to get any busier. You take your time and enjoy your breakfast, then I'll drive you home."

She left to serve other tables, and stopped to joke with a pair of truck drivers who'd just come in. Kohl watched her as he ate. He wanted to know so much more about this woman. He was surprised that connecting with her had been as easy as it had, and worried that he was nothing more than a temporary distraction, someone new and different from the men who were regulars at the grill. From what he'd seen, most of them were truck drivers and he assumed that many of them drove scheduled routes that brought them through here often.

Just as he finished his bacon and eggs and was about to take a bite of the last piece of toast, Cara walked up behind him and put a hand on his shoulder. "If you're finished, I'm ready to go," she said softly. "I'll pick up your dishes and then we're out of here! Okay?"

She went to the back and got a tray for the dishes, and when she returned Kohl slid out from behind the table and stood. He reached in for the axe, picked up the pail and walked behind her as she took the tray of dirty dishes to the back. She waved for him to follow and they left through the back door and went straight to the parking lot.

"My steed awaits," she said, pointing to an old Jeep at the far side of the lot.

"Don't believe I've ever rode a steed before. Should I be worried?"

"Two year old can do it. Besides, this one is pretty tame. Trust me. I keep it under control."

"We're off, then," Kohl said, as he climbed in beside her and pulled the door shut.

The Jeep's canvas top was torn around the doors and windows, so that a constant stream of icy wind poured in as she drove. The windshield quickly fogged over as their warm breath made contact with the cold glass. Kohl tried to wipe a clear spot with his hand so that she could see where she was going.

"I could almost drive this road blind," Cara said. "Which is a good thing, because you ain't helping much."

"Sorry. I'm doing the best I can."

She laughed. "Don't take me so serious," she said. "Anyway, we're getting a little bit of heat now and the defrosters ought to kick in pretty soon. One good thing about this old horse is, it warms up pretty fast."

"You drive this way all the time?"

"This way? You mean slow?"

"No, I mean do you drive this road?"

"At least twice a day for the last two years."

"Then you've been going right by my house. It's up ahead. On the left."

"That old farm house with the big trees behind it?"

"That's it."

"How about that! I thought somebody lived there, though. There was an old van parked there most of the time. But I guess it's been a while since I seen it."

She'd barely finished speaking before they were within sight of the house. "That's it," Kohl said. "Can you come in for a minute? I'd like for you to meet my dog."

Cara pulled over and stopped, the Jeep barely off the road and facing on-coming traffic. Kohl opened the door on his side and slid out, then reached behind the seat to retrieve his axe and the pail. Cara came around and took the axe and he led her around the side of the house to the back door. Inside, Jake was barking furiously.

"Sounds like you got yourself a pretty good watch dog," Cara said.

"He'll be one of the best, after he gets healthy and has time to learn a few things."

Kohl held the door open and she stepped inside, leaned the axe against the wall, and extended her hands, palms down, to the dog. Jake stopped barking and stared at the newcomer as if uncertain her presence was acceptable. Kohl, meanwhile, had set the pail down and lifted the dog food from it. He ripped open the bag and dropped a handful of the dry pellets on the floor. Jake sprang to the food and began to slurp it up like liquid.

"Whoa, there," Kohl said. "Don't choke yourself. There's plenty more where that came from."

Cara stood aside and watched the man and the dog. Kohl poured more of the pellets on the floor and Jake gobbled them up and whined for more. Kohl dumped a large mound of the food before him, laughing, feeling good because he could feed the famished animal until it was sated. He poured yet another serving and finally

Jake's ravenous hunger looked to be satisfied. The dog crept into the living room and lay down on the old mattress before the fireplace.

"We shared the bed last night," Kohl said. "That helped us keep warm."

Cara looked about, shaking her head. "You can't live like this," she said. "Not when the weather gets worse. You'll freeze to death. You and the dog both."

"I'll get the place fixed up."

"But you don't have no heat."

"The fireplace works pretty good and there's still wood in the back yard. Now that I've got an axe I can chop more. These old walls are thick, too, and keep out a lot of the cold. I think we can make it."

Cara shook her head. "Listen to me, Kohl," she said firmly. "It's going to take a ton of work to fix this place up. You could spend all your time chopping wood and you'd still barely have enough to get by. You haven't got a car, and don't tell me that old mattress gives you a good night's sleep!"

"I know you're right, but this place isn't so bad compared to where I lived for the last twenty years. Cara, there's something I need to tell you, something you don't—"

She waved a hand and interrupted. "I already know where you were for the last twenty years. Danny Connor filled me in pretty good on all that."

"I should have figured on somebody telling you. Danny's been decent about it—not like some other people I've run into."

"I doubt you expected they'd welcome you back with a parade and fireworks, though. Most people ain't too quick to forget and forgive."

"Yeah, well. I'm not looking for special treatment. All I want is a chance to prove myself. But I want you to hear my side of the story, you know, since there's a lot of it Danny Connor and nobody else around here could tell you, even if they wanted to."

She fixed her eyes on him in an intense stare. "If you did anything to hurt a woman or an animal, Kohl, I'm not interested in your story," she said firmly. "If you just busted up some louse of a guy who probably deserved it, okay, I will. You'll get a chance to tell me soon enough. But look, I've got to move along now. There's a bunch of stuff I need to get done while I have time off. I'll see you again soon?"

Kohl wanted to thank her for both the companionship and the ride home, but he always felt awkward trying to express gratitude. He settled for giving a direct answer to her question.

"Yes, I really hope so," he said, as Cara turned and started toward the door.

Their movement roused Jake from his full-bellied lethargy. He ran to catch up.

When Cara pulled the door open, they were hit by a rush of cold air that was like a hard slap across the nose. Jake crowded close to Kohl's legs and Cara pulled her coat more tightly around her body. They'd barely rounded the corner of the house when she stopped suddenly. Kohl was looking ahead and almost bumped into her.

"Oh, crap!" she exclaimed. "Can you believe this?"

Deputy Scott Sobeski sat slouched in his patrol car, which he had backed close to the front of Cara's Jeep, almost touching bumpers. The car's engine was running and the driver's window was down. His eyes were fixed on them in a cold stare as they approached.

"I want to talk to you, Kohl," Sobeski demanded as they drew near.

Kohl stepped close to the car. "All right," he said, "talk."

"Where were you last night around ten o'clock?"

"I was here. Why?"

"Somebody with a description that matched yours got into a fight at Shelby's bar and broke a man's jaw. You're on parole, Kohl. A little activity like that could put you right back behind bars. I don't suppose there are any witnesses to your whereabouts last night?" Sobeski looked directly at Cara.

"Just me and my dog," Kohl said. "But you know it wasn't me."

"Seen your parole officer yet?"

"I haven't been assigned one. But you know that, too."

"Damn you, Sobeski," Cara flared. "Ain't you got nothing better to do than harass innocent people? Move your damned car so I can go!"

"Oh, yeah, I'm leaving," the deputy said. "But if I were you I'd be more careful who I hung out with. Lie down with dogs you're likely to get up with fleas. But I expect you've laid down with enough dogs to know that."

Before she could reply, Sobeski gunned the patrol car back onto the road. They watched as the vehicle crested a slight hill and disappeared from view. Cara was livid with anger. Kohl took her hand. "Listen to me," he said, "Sobeski's out to get me and I'm not sure how far he might go. I don't want to get you in trouble for hanging out with me. Okay?"

She laughed, but it was an expression of derision, not humor.

"That little prick's too big a coward to do anything but talk," she said. "Us being together works both ways, Kohl. Sobeski's been hitting on me ever since I come here and he won't take it lightly seeing me with another guy. You know what I mean?"

He nodded. "Yes, I do. He may be watching you as much as he's watching me. That's not good for either one of us."

Kohl and Jake stood beside the road as Cara got into the Jeep and drove away. He reached down and scuffed the dog's head. "Let's get back in out of this cold," he said. "And I've got an axe now, buddy. We'll get to some serious wood-chopping pretty soon."

SIX

ONCE BACK INSIDE the old house, Kohl was abruptly overtaken by a wave of loneliness. Time with Cara had offered a glimpse of what a normal way of life could be like. This was what he wanted, but this was not what he had. An empty house was not a home.

Jake sat and waited, as if expecting him to set a new plan in motion. Kohl sat down on the cold floor beside the dog and gave him a pat on the head.

"You and me are pretty much family now, Jake," he said. "I know you won't desert me, and I'll never let you down. I've never told anyone this before, but I've been lonely most of my life. I never had many friends. Angie was the only one who was ever really close, like somebody I'd tell my secrets to. You're my best friend now, and I'll tell you my secrets if you'll tell me yours. How 'bout it? We got a deal?"

Tears suddenly welled up in Kohl's eyes. Jake apparently noticed, and moved closer, squirming around until his head lay across Kohl's thigh. In a matter of minutes the dog was fast asleep.

Kohl sat a while longer. He did not want to bother Jake, and he was not eager to get out into the woodlot and start swinging an axe. When he finally did start to get up, he gently took Jake's head in his hands and moved it off his leg and lowered it carefully to the floor. Jake showed no sign of being disturbed.

On impulse, he went upstairs and looked about, wondering who might have slept in these rooms during the years he was away. The girl at the farm supply store, Amy, said kids had used the house for partying. He'd seen no sign of this here on the second floor and he was grateful, glad not to have had his mother's bedroom defiled the way the living room had been and, to a lesser extent, the kitchen.

He went to the room that had been his and checked under the loose floor plank in the closet. His money had not been disturbed. He hadn't been worried about it, and looked for no reason other than a habit formed years ago.

The closet itself was filled with memories of youthful adventure. He had made it home base for all the intrigues and conspiracies his fertile young mind could dream up. Nothing that germinated in his own imagination could compete with a discovery that was completely accidental, though, and it was both embarrassing and funny when he recalled it now. After all the years that had come and gone, it still was his secret, never revealed to another living being.

Probably without knowing, whoever built this house had partitioned second-floor rooms in such a way that space between certain walls magnified sound like a speaker box. Young Ernst had discovered that, lying quietly on the floor of this closet, he could hear his sisters' conversations almost as clearly as he could have if he shared their room.

What he heard was boring only when they talked about him, and this seldom happened. Mostly, they talked about other boys.

In the years since, Kohl had kicked himself many times after realizing that things his sisters said probably were typical of other girls, as well. Had he understood this earlier, he might have had vastly different expectations when it came to Angie. Sometimes his sisters talked like sex-starved vixens. They discussed things they wanted to do with certain boys and schemed to make these happen. He counted all this as "pretend" talk, though, and it never crossed his young and naïve mind that it might represent actual desires.

He missed his sisters terribly. They always had his back when he was little, and as he grew older he could tell they relished his good days and hurt for his bad ones just as much as his mother did.

Ada had visited him at The Pines a few times. The prison environment must have been awfully oppressive to her, and her visits usually turned into unpleasant occasions, anyway. At least indirectly, she always got around to the humiliation he had brought upon his family and how painful it was to see the effects of his terrible deed on his mother.

Hannah had come only once, and that was to bring his mother

to visit. Hannah, herself, never entered the visitors' area. His mother kept saying that his sister would be along in a few minutes, but Hannah never showed.

He sat on the floor beside the closet door longer than he'd intended to and spent most of this time reliving unpleasant memories. He had no desire to go out into the cold, but finally gave in to necessity. If he didn't get more firewood it would be impossible to have any heat at all in the old house for more than a few hours. Somewhat reluctantly, he went downstairs and got his axe and headed to the woodlot.

He had no plan, but started out by chopping vigorously at the worst underbrush to make clear working space around three fallen branches. If the wood was rotten, it wouldn't burn well in the fireplace. The long white oak limbs had not been on the ground too long and were still solid. Chopping these into short lengths proved much more arduous than he'd expected, though, and he quickly grasped the fact that his wood-chopping skill was more limited than he'd expected. Swinging an axe clearly used shoulder and arm muscles not accustomed to heavy demands, and in what seemed to Kohl no time at all he was nearly exhausted. He took a break and went inside.

Jake waited in the kitchen.

"I can't believe you're hungry already," he teased. "What have you done to work off that full belly, anyway?"

Jake cocked his head and stared in a way that suggested immense curiosity. The animal's serious expression brought a smile to Kohl's face. He reached down, scuffed Jake on the head, and then retrieved the bag of dog food from a corner of the room and poured him another meal. Jake dug in, as usual, like he was starving.

After checking on the fireplace, Kohl went back outside and pumped fresh water into the new pail and brought it back to the kitchen. He poured some in Jake's pan and set it on the floor.

"I think you can manage from here," he said, scuffing the dog's head again. "I've got to get back to work."

He went back to the woodlot, determined to finish the chore he'd started. It was mind over matter and he worked mechanically, beginning to feel some rhythm in the swing of the axe. In time he was able to carry in five armloads of good quality firewood. He dropped the first two of these on the kitchen floor, then decided to take the rest into the living room and stack the small logs nearer the fireplace so that it would be close when it was needed.

"Use your head and save your heels, Kohl," he said in the general direction of Jake, lying on the mattress but not asleep. "That's what my mother used to say. 'Use your head and save your heels.' Good advice, wouldn't you say? That's okay. You don't have to answer. It's just that I value your opinion, you know."

Kohl was tired. He wasn't used to strenuous activity like chopping wood and he hadn't had a solid night's sleep for nearly a month. Even in the familiar surroundings of his prison cell, he had lain awake for hours during the night—too excited to sleep because he was about to be released, his mind crowded with memories of home and worries about what he'd find there. Bittersweet reminiscences of times with Angie became a burden, and grief over his mother and questions about his sisters and the house they'd left for him intensified until they felt like a curse. And, without fail, there was endless self-examination about how he could have done what he did twenty years ago, an act never intended and monstrously out of character.

He was hungry, too. He got the last can of beans from the kitchen, opened it with his new can opener, and ate the beans cold, directly from the container. He rinsed the empty can over the kitchen sink with water from the pail he'd brought in earlier. The water tasted good and he drank all the can held.

Outside, the wind sighed softly as it rounded the corners of the old house and rippled through the bare branches of the oak trees. Kohl found modest comfort in the sound. This was something familiar, something known and understood. He remembered the windbreak of densely planted pine trees that once stood along the west side of the home site, but these trees apparently had been cut and their stumps pulled from the ground to clear another few feet of the fertile farmland by which the place was surrounded. Kohl wondered who owned that property now, what might happen to it in the years to come. He was not sure where his land ended and someone else's began. But this was not an issue of sufficient consequence to keep him awake. He soon joined Jake in a sound though restless sleep.

Danny Connor was at the kitchen door. It was still early, a pale sun losing its battle to provide noticeable warmth. Kohl had just stoked the burnt-out embers in the fireplace and thrown on more wood, waking Jake in the process. Jake sounded the first alarm that someone was outside.

"I hope I'm not too early," Danny Connor said when Kohl opened the door. "I didn't figure you'd be sleeping in, given the circumstances. I didn't know you had a dog."

"Jake's my new best friend," Kohl said. "And, yeah, I've been getting up early for twenty years when it didn't matter, but if I slept too late here me and Jake probably would both freeze to death. Come in, Danny. I'm sorry I don't have any hot coffee to offer you."

"Already had mine. I just left work an hour or so ago. I wanted to talk to you about something, and I thought catching you here would be the best place to do it."

Kohl's defenses shot up at once. Somebody wanting to talk usually meant trouble. Although he'd come to think he was going to like Danny Connor, the little contact they'd had hadn't given him any reason to think that Danny might be an exception. "Here suits me," he said somewhat rudely. "So go ahead and talk."

"You're going to need somebody on your side, Kohl. I'm betting you face some tough sledding. I may not have a whole lot to offer, but I talked to Jack—Jack Gengler, you may remember him, he's the manager—I talked to Jack and he said we could hire you part-time if you need a job. It won't be anything high class, and it won't pay a lot. Probably washing dishes on the night shift. But Jack said he'd keep you on until you could find decent work someplace else."

Kohl was too surprised to have a quick answer. But he needed a job desperately, and no matter what happened he would be eternally grateful to Danny Connor.

"I don't know what to say, Danny," he said. "I didn't expect anything like this. Sure, I need a job. I don't care what it is. I mean . . . look, you didn't have to do this for me. I won't forget it."

Danny Connor smiled. "I hope you still feel that way some night when the heat goes out at the grill and you're standing back in the dismal cold-room up to your elbows in greasy dishwater," he said. "The sinks and dish racks are in the cold-room, meaning it was meant for storage. Don't mean it's refrigerated, but there's no extra heat back there. Anyhow, Jack's the one you have to thank. I couldn't have done anything if he didn't sign on to it."

"Maybe so. But you had to bring it up. I owe you, Danny, big time."

Danny Connor's face reddened. "I always admired you in high school," he said. "You always seemed to stick to your principles. I don't remember you ever selling anybody out to suit your own whims. Yeah, I know, that was a long time ago, but that's the kind of thing you remember for a long time. I told Jack he'd always get his money's worth out of you."

The two men talked for a full hour, much of that time spent reminiscing about their high school days. Kohl was embarrassed that Danny Connor remembered a lot more about him than he did about Danny. Trying to compensate, he mentioned tryouts for the football team where Danny was selected and Kohl was not. Danny Connor said Kohl was lucky; football practice every night and a game every weekend took their toll on classroom performance. But he loved the game and still believed that Michigan football, especially, helped kids learn to handle tough but fair competition.

Danny Connor said he needed to go. He hadn't planned to take this much of Kohl's time. He said Kohl should come to the Purple Onion whenever it was convenient and talk with Jack Gengler about a work schedule.

"Some of them night shifts drag pretty slow," he said. "We may have lots of time to talk football, which suits me just fine. Not a lot of guys still around who remember the teams I played on."

Danny's smile disappeared and he lowered his voice. "One other thing I need to tell you," he said. "Watch out for Sobeski. He's a nasty little man who likes to run over people. Don't give him an excuse to run over you."

"Yeah," Kohl answered, "I've seen enough to have him pegged already. Robocop. Probably writes up little kids for having their shoes on the wrong feet and feels proud of hisself for protecting society. I don't figure him as a local. Where in the hell did he come from, anyway?"

"Detroit. Remember Robert Hightower, the half-Chippewa kid we went to high school with?"

"Sure. Little Bobby Hightower. I went to school with him since first grade."

"He's a deputy sheriff now. I talk to him pretty regular. He says Sobeski was a cop in Detroit and got his ass kicked off the force there. Says his mom's family comes from around here, going back a couple of generations, and had pull with the sheriff. He was slipped into a deputy slot without a whole lot of attention paid to his background, is what Robert said."

"It works the same everywhere. It's all politics. The big dog's going to come out on top, whatever it takes. Always has little dogs to lick up after it. Get in the way and the rats will be feeding on your body in a trash bin in some dark alley."

Danny Connor laughed. "May be a little exaggerated, but I don't quarrel with your point," he said. "You probably heard some stories up there, meaning no offense."

"None taken," Kohl replied. "Like I said, it's all politics."

"Just don't cross him, Kohl."

"That's good advice I don't need, but thanks, Danny."

"Sure. No problem. And I got one other thing you may or may not be interested in. I know you don't have transportation, but it can't be more than half a mile from here to the truck stop and it's a good road. We had two or three old bikes laying around and I brought you one. It's yours if you want it. May not be high class, but sure beats walking."

Kohl couldn't hold back a laugh. "That might be the best present I ever got," he said. "Danny Connor, you'd make somebody a good grandma! That's the kind of thing a grandma would have come up with, you know what I'm saying? I appreciate it, man. I truly do."

Danny already had gone to his truck to unload the bicycle.

Kohl tried to remember Jack Gengler. The name was familiar but he couldn't put a face with it. Danny hadn't given him much to go on besides a name. But why worry about this now. I'll find out what kind of man he is soon enough, he thought. *And I hope he's good. I need the job, but I won't be pushed around.*

SEVEN

DANNY CONNOR HAD given Kohl a second reason to hurry to the Purple Onion. He wanted to see Jack Gengler before he had time to change his mind. The sooner he could get his name on a payroll, the better. Even if only for a few hours a week. And he also hoped that inquiring promptly would demonstrate the work ethic Danny apparently had promised the manager. He owed this much to Danny.

But Kohl already had admitted to himself that he was eager to get to the grill whether he talked with Jack Gengler or not. Cara would be there.

He fed Jake, heated a pan of water on the edge of the fireplace, and went upstairs to the bathroom and shaved and bathed as completely as practical under the circumstances. He could see enough of his own image in the mirror to recognize that he was as disheveled as a vagabond. His pants and shirt were wrinkled worse than he'd thought, clear evidence that he had been sleeping in his clothes. He simply would have to risk being offensive to Jack Gengler. Cara wouldn't be surprised by his appearance.

Back downstairs, he let Jake out and added enough wood to the fireplace to maintain at least a moderate level of heat while he was gone. Jake barked at the door after only a few minutes, announcing to anyone who cared that he'd had enough of the cold and was ready to be back inside. As soon as he was in, Kohl pushed Danny Connor's old bicycle out to the road and headed toward town. Old Church Road was rough riding in spots, but what had seemed a long walk was a surprisingly short ride.

Jack Gengler wasn't there when he got to the Purple Onion, but

Cara was. She greeted Kohl with a warm hug and led him to a table near the back.

"Jack don't get here before noon some days," she said, "but he's bound to be here sooner or later. Let me get you some breakfast while you wait. Have any problem getting away from Jake?"

"You know Jake. Throw a little food his way and he's satisfied. He probably was asleep again before I was in the seat of my new bicycle."

It was the first time Cara had heard about the bicycle. She found it a great story, funny for "a tale about two grown men." But she was happy that Kohl had wheels. Like Danny Connor said, it beat walking, especially with winter coming on. And the best part was the fact that he would be making this trip often once he got a work schedule.

As business picked up, Cara quickly got too busy to sit and talk. Kohl was left alone to finish his breakfast and reflect on what lay ahead. He already had begun to consider the difference a modest income could make in his life. For starters, he might worry less about running out of money. That had been a big concern from the minute he walked out of his cell and set out for home. He worried about it night and day, even more so now that he'd seen the price of things. And now he had Jake to feed.

But life had taught him not to count on anything before it was in his hands. Hadn't he learned his lesson twenty years ago? Hadn't a carefree existence and the promise of a happy future been jerked away and possibly denied him forever? Until his first payday he would not think any more about how to spend new income.

It was almost noon when Jack Gengler finally showed up. Cara brought him to Kohl and made quick, informal introductions. Gengler did not look familiar.

"Danny told me good things about you," Gengler said. "Danny's word is good enough for me. Come to work Monday night, say about ten p.m. Welcome to the family."

They shook hands and Jack Gengler was gone, disappearing into his tiny office and closing the door. Cara had kept herself close by. She rushed over to where Kohl sat, making no effort to hide her eagerness.

"So?" she demanded.

"So I guess I come to work Monday night. That's all I know. He didn't even mention money."

"Jack's a good guy. He'll be fair. I'm happy for you, Kohl. But I wish we could be working the same shift. You'll probably be gone before I get here in the morning. Look, I'm finished for the day. Come throw your fancy bicycle in the back of my Jeep and I'll give you a ride home."

Kohl was in favor of anything that would keep him close to her a little longer. He also welcomed the ride. He'd been away longer than he expected, and he was concerned about Jake. It would be cold in the old house and the dog would be hungry, and Kohl couldn't remember whether he had left him water. Besides, he didn't look forward to being back out in the cold and pedaling against the wind on Danny Connor's old bicycle.

He needn't have worried. When they got to the old house, Jake was asleep in front of the fireplace. The fire had burned out but the room still was warm. There was a pan of water on the kitchen floor, and if Jake was hungry he didn't show it when he woke. He got up slowly and greeted Kohl with a nuzzle around the ankles and brief eye contact and then stood against Cara's leg waiting for a stroke on the head. She promptly obliged.

"I'm not even sure he missed me," Kohl said. "It looks to me like Mr. Lazybones has been asleep all day."

Cara put a hand on his arm. "I want you to come home with me," she said. "I've got an extra room where you and Jake can stay as long as you need to. My place ain't fancy, but it's warm. And I'm lonely, Kohl. I've been by myself for a long time. You ever been lonely?"

"Yes."

"No living being likes to be alone. Not all the time. Not even the animals."

"I know I don't, but I can't speak for the animals."

"Papa always said wolves run in packs for company. We'd lay in the grass just before dark and watch the birds play in the wind and he'd always point out the couples. I think they were crows, but he'd tell us they were eagles. Unless he was in a bad mood, then he called them filthy buzzards."

Kohl laughed. "Whatever. I wouldn't know a buzzard from a turkey."

"But you know what I mean?"

"Sure. I don't like being lonely any more than anybody else does."

"So you coming, or what?"

"I don't know what to say. You kinda took me by surprise. Are you sure?"

"I'm sure. Get your stuff together and load it in the Jeep. And let's be damn sure we don't forget Jake's food. Me and Jake are going to be good friends, too, and I don't mind having a good watch dog. Okay?"

Kohl still was hesitant. "I wasn't sure you'd like Jake," he said. "I didn't know if you liked dogs, or not."

"Well, there's lots about me you don't know just like there's lots about you I don't know. If we don't make too big a deal about trying to find out everything all at once we ought to get along all right. Get your stuff."

It took only minutes for them to sort out Kohl's few personal items and pack them in the new five-gallon plastic pail he used for carrying water from the well. He went upstairs and retrieved his cash from the hiding place beneath the loose closet floor board. He made no effort to hide the money when he came back down and she showed no interest in it.

"Just lock this place up and forget about it for now," Cara said.

"Nope. I can't. Maybe you didn't notice, but there's no lock on the back door. Why do you think I got this vicious watch dog?"

"So I'll feel a lot safer, too. Ready?"

They took the bicycle out of the Jeep, and when Kohl signaled with his hand Jake clambered obediently into the back seat. They stowed the pail and the bag of dog food and climbed in, pulling the canvas doors shut and latching them against the angry wind. Cara started the engine. She turned on the heater and defroster fan, rotating the knob to its highest setting, but the engine was cold and the fan blasted frigid air into the cabin.

"Jesus god it's cold," Cara said. "Why does anybody want to live up here?"

"Michigan? Because it's a real pleasant place in July and August," he said, not entirely in jest. Then, more seriously, "Yeah, I guess there are places where the winter's not so bad, but I wouldn't know about them. Michigan's the only place I've ever lived."

"Poor baby."

"So how 'bout you? Where do Irish Travelers live before they come to Michigan?"

"All over, I guess, but probably mostly in the South. When we're out stealing chickens and all the other stuff we're accused of, we like to do it in warm weather."

Her mood, like Kohl's, had brightened.

"But I thought it was the gypsies who are supposed to steal chickens, and you said Irish Travelers aren't gypsies."

"But people think we are. Maybe going under a different brand name, like an old Ford pretending to be a Mercury."

"Did you live in the South?"

"Yes, when I was a little girl. We lived in Alabama and Papa was a huckster man. He drove around to the country houses and sold things from a truck. Mostly groceries, but some little hardware things too. I don't think he made much money, but we got by."

"Where'd you live?"

"For two years we lived in a van—a converted bread truck, I think. A poor folks' motor home."

"Cooking, sleeping, everything?"

"Yeah, sure. Everything. It had a little kerosene stove my momma cooked on. And bunk beds in the back. My daddy and momma slept in the one on the bottom and my brother and me slept in the one on top."

"You didn't have much privacy, living like that."

"No shit! We'd lay there and listen to them screwing. Seemed like every night. They tried to be quiet, but the bed squeaked. It took them forever sometimes. Papa had a way of grunting at the end and momma made a little sound more like a whine. By the time they finished my brother would be all aroused and was always squashing me against the wall."

Her openness caught Kohl by surprise. He fumbled for words, but had no idea how to reply.

Cara seemed to sense that she'd left him in an awkward situation. She put her hand on his arm and laughed. "It wasn't like you think," she said. "We were just little kids. You know, six and eight years old or something like that. I don't go around making excuses for myself saying I was molested by my brother."

"I wasn't thinking that. I mean—"

"Anyway," she interrupted, "we're just about home. The exciting story of the life of your favorite Irish Traveler will have to be continued some other time."

She turned into a narrow lane almost obscured by overhanging branches. It was lined on both sides by cherry orchards, their trees starkly bare. Some hundred yards off the road sat a dilapidated trailer which Kohl guessed to be no more than forty feet long. There was a gravel pad in front and she stopped the Jeep right at the door.

"Maybe it don't look like much, but it's home," she said. "You guys come on in."

Once inside, Cara grasped Kohl by the arm and spun herself around so that they were face-to-face. "Now put that dog in the other room and come to bed," she demanded. "I need you, Kohl. Bad. You wouldn't believe how long it's been since I've been with a man." She began to tug at her boots, urgency in every move.

Kohl stepped awkwardly toward the back of the trailer, then turned and signaled Jake. The dog slunk forward, wagging its tail furiously, and Kohl nudged it into the tiny room and slid the door shut. Jake whined once, softly, and grew quiet.

Cara had almost finished undressing. As he went to her she seized the front of his shirt and began to undo the buttons.

It was over quickly. Cara giggled. "God, that was great," she said. "I needed it. Sorry if I come across as desperate, though to tell you the truth I was. Sort of."

"Thank you," Kohl said.

"Thank you? For what?"

"Well, you know, for what we did."

"For what we did? You don't thank a woman after you've had sex, Kohl. I wasn't doing you a favor."

"I'm sorry . . . I mean . . ."

"Forget it."

"Cara, I want to tell you something."

"So? Tell me."

"That was the first time I ever had sex. I guess I wasn't very good."

She raised herself on an elbow and looked at him incredulously. "You're shitting me, right?"

"No. That was the first time."

"How old are you, Kohl?"

"Forty-one."

"You're forty-one years old and you expect me to believe that you never had sex before?"

Kohl could feel the blood creeping up his neck and into his face. But if he was embarrassed it was his own fault. It wasn't Cara who committed the act that sent him to prison. "You have to remember, I've been out of circulation for the last twenty years," he said.

"So how about all that butt stuff in prison? Is it like we see in the movies?"

"No, not like that. It happens, usually with a prison wolf, but anybody who doesn't want to get into that stuff doesn't have to. That was my experience, anyhow."

"I don't know the language, you know. What's a prison wolf?"

"Sorry. There are guys who like it. Guys who swing both ways. And there always is the slave—a guy who's scared and latches onto somebody for protection. They do whatever their big man wants."

"And you didn't get raped in the shower by some big, scary black dude?"

Kohl laughed. "Nope," he said, "it didn't happen to me. I'm not saying it don't happen, but not to everybody, like they show in the movies."

She was silent for a moment. "Not to pluck a dead chicken, but you would have been twenty before they sent you up. Look, I'm not prying into things that are none of my business. You lived your life and I lived mine. Let's let it go at that, okay?"

"But I want to tell you something you don't know. What really happened that nobody knows about. You said you'd listen if I wanted to talk about it. Remember?"

"I know. And I will. Can't we put it off for now, though? If it's real sticky stuff I might want a drink or something before I hear it."

"Yes, it can wait."

Cara smiled. "There's one thing I do need to know about you right now, though. Don't you have a first name?"

"Yes, but I hate it."

"Jesus, Kohl. It can't be that bad. What is your name, anyway?"

"My name is Ernst Kohl. I was named after my grandfather."

"Nothing wrong with that. I'll call you whatever you like. If you want to go by Kohl, that's what I'll call you."

"When I started seventh grade, a school bully always called me 'Little Hitler.' That's one reason I hate my name so much."

"Bullies are the worst. We all had them one time or another. I always thought if I was a boy I'd beat them all up. But I got another question. What in the hell is that little tattoo on your back supposed to mean? I don't get the numbers."

Kohl felt himself blushing again. "It's a prison thing," he said. "Guys inside know what it means. I was still a kid and they made me do it. Or, I ought to say, they did it to me. Two guys held me down and another one tattooed me with a bent paperclip and ashes from some paper they burned. He mixed it with butter or something. It got infected, but I survived. It's permanent."

"God almighty, that's crude."

"Yeah, well. They told me it's supposed to be a badge of honor or something. You know, a brotherhood kind of thing."

Cara frowned. "So is that what the numbers mean? Like a gang symbol?"

Kohl laughed, surprising himself. He had never thought there was anything funny about his tattoo. "It's simple," he said. "The numbers are thirteen and a half. It means twelve jurors and one judge gave me half a chance."

"I get it. Probably some big con man thought that up. But thanks for telling me about it. Now let's go take care of Jake."

They left the bedroom and Cara stopped in the cramped kitchen while Kohl went to the back and let Jake come out to join them. She had taken a large bowl down from a cabinet over the sink and poured a generous helping of Jake's dry food into it.

"He oughtn't to be hungry yet," Kohl said. "Not after what he had back at the house."

"You ever had a dog before? Dogs are always hungry." She stooped and put the bowl on the floor. "Besides, I wanted to feed him. Me and Jake are going to be good friends and the best way to start is to give him food."

As if he wanted to prove her correct, Jake hit the bowl like an animal that hadn't been fed for a week. He gobbled up the food and licked the bowl, lay down on his belly with his front legs extended, and wagged his tail in a motion that swept the floor like some kind of mechanical broom.

Cara said they should bathe the dog in the shower. Kohl resisted, but she was adamant. A dog's dirt was no worse than people's dirt, and anyway the shower stall was easy to clean. Just run the shower a minute and rinse it down. And by the way, since they were on the topic, she expected Kohl to get a good shower, himself. She doubted he'd had one back at the cold house.

Jake took to soap and water the same way he had welcomed food. When he was clean and as dry as they could manage they applied some of the salve Kohl had picked up at the farm supply store, rubbing it onto the visible areas of irritated skin. By the time this was done, Jake was ready for another nap.

"He can have the bed in that little back room," Cara said. "You're going to sleep with me."

Since Kohl already was partially undressed, she took his clothes and put them in the washing machine. He had clean underwear, but his pants and shirt were dirty and wrinkled. They would have to buy him more as soon as possible, she announced, but in the meantime her laundry was his to use. "My men have to look first class," she joked, and Kohl forced a laugh, even though he didn't find this funny.

But he was beginning to feel comfortable with this woman, sharing a level of intimacy he couldn't have imagined just hours before. They talked away the afternoon. Cara told stories about her childhood in the South, with vivid descriptions he found fascinating. He talked about his sisters and his mother. He told her about George Spencer giving him a ride and asked if she had seen the newspaper reports of his coming. She said she didn't read the papers, but she heard talk in the grill. She paid no attention to what she heard, though, and wouldn't have known what the big fuss was all about.

Jake slept for a time in the back room. When he joined them later, he made clear that he was ready for another snack. Cara got a bowl from the cupboard and poured more dog food.

"I want him to love me, too," she said. "Most all animals get close real fast to anybody that feeds them, and dogs and cats fall in love with anybody they get close to. He already loves you, Kohl. See the way he looks at you? You can read a dog's eyes as easy as you can read a headline in the *Gazette*."

Kohl couldn't help but laugh. "I thought you didn't read the *Gazette*," he teased.

"I don't read the little print, but people leave copies in the Purple Onion and sometimes I do glance at what's front-page news. Just the headlines. That's all I have time for."

"Cara, how much do you know about Sobeski? Is he dangerous or just bluff?"

"Sobeski? I'd say both. He's too much of a coward to be real dangerous, but one of these days he's going to back hisself in a corner with one of his big bluffs, and you know about cornered animals. He could be dangerous. Stay away from him if you can."

"I'd be real glad to stay away from him," Kohl told her. "Problem is, he's not going to stay away from me. Like they say in the pen, you do a 'chin check.' That means you punch a guy in the face to see if he'll fight back. Sobeski wants to provoke me into fighting back."

"He won't back off you. And don't trust him to play fair. Sobeski don't believe in rules for him, just rules for everybody else."

It was still daylight outside when Cara announced that she was ready for bed. Kohl could see through the pretext that she had to be up early in the morning because of her work schedule at the grill. He knew there was an ulterior motive. And it was a motive he found immensely exciting, but at the same time somewhat intimidating. Until today, Ernst Kohl had never considered the possibility that a woman might take the lead and initiate sex.

EIGHT

KOHL WOKE IN the morning alone in the bed with Jake barking just outside the bedroom door. He got up quickly, feeling foolish for having overslept, and opened the door to welcome the dog. There was no sign of Cara. He called her name but there was no response. Jake turned and ran to the kitchen and the bag of dog food sitting in a corner.

"It always makes me feel good to see that it's my chow that's of interest and not my company," he teased Jake. "But don't worry. I'm not a man to hold grudges. Sorry to be late with your breakfast, but we've got the good stuff now and I'll get you a big bowl of it as soon as I find a bowl."

He opened the door of the nearest overhead cabinet, but it was the place Cara kept her plates and saucers. A shelf in the next cabinet held soup and cereal bowls and Kohl took the largest one and set it on the counter. He stooped and picked up the bag of dog food and poured a generous helping for Jake.

"See, just like I promised," he said as he put the bowl on the floor. The dog attacked the food as if he hadn't had a bite to eat in days.

"And you don't have to worry about last night, Jake. The fact that I shared a bed with Cara doesn't mean she's about to take your place. No, nope, no way! Just won't happen."

Kohl got down on his knees to be nearer Jake's eye level. Jake's attention was aimed directly at the food bowl, though, and he didn't look up.

"You look good all cleaned up," he said seriously. "And it must be some kind of miracle, because you even smell good!" He ignored the dog's lack of interest and kept on talking. "You and me are more than just buddies, Jake. We're family. That means we're always there for each other. And we stick together, okay?"

Jake demanded a second helping. He gulped it down, too, and it wasn't until after he'd licked the bowl clean that he apparently decided it was time to pay attention to the only human in the room. He looked Kohl in the eyes with an expression little short of adulation. Kohl scuffed his head and stroked him down the back. "Who's the smartest, toughest dog there ever was? Jake, you say? Why, of course it's Jake!"

The dog apparently had found his favored spot in Cara's trailer during the night—a fluffy white rug lying directly in front of a heat vent in the other bedroom. He started toward it, stopped and looked back at Kohl, then ambled on. Kohl told himself that his presence probably was not needed back there. Instead of following the dog, he went back to the room he had shared with Cara.

On the foot of the bed where he should have seen it earlier was a note addressed to "Dear Friend Kohl," written on the back of an order form from the Purple Onion Grill. He moved closer to a window for more reading light.

"Some of us have to work," Cara had written, "but I don't mind when I know there will be somebody waiting for me at home when my shift is done. Please help yourself to any food or drink you find. And don't worry, cowboy. You gave me a good ride!!!!"

The note was signed, "Gypsy Woman."

Kohl read it a second time, aloud. He found it funny but also a bit scary. What Cara had written was a straightforward testament to her obvious assumption that the two of them might continue living together. He hadn't considered this.

Although he had been immensely attracted to Cara, sleeping with her had left him with curiously mixed feelings. His first night in bed with a woman had been all that he could have imagined. Cara would always be his first partner in lovemaking, and he was sure he would recall the details tenderly for as long as he lived. But all he could think of just now was Angie. How he had longed to make love to her, yet settled for the beautiful vision of eventually having her as best friend, wife, and lover for life. That fantasy might be dead in his logical mind, but in his subconscious it still was very much alive. In his dreams, his desire for Angie played out time and again in acts of passion.

Jake apparently had changed his mind, meanwhile, and decided he wanted Kohl's company more than he wanted to go back to bed. He whined softly at the door.

Kohl opened the door and Jake showed his appreciation by wagging his tail with great enthusiasm. It was almost as if his whole body had to move to accomplish this, and almost immediately he was fully into what Kohl had come to call his "love dance." Kohl got down on the floor with the dog and hugged it tightly against him. Jake's movement subsided as quickly as it had begun and his body relaxed. It was as if Kohl's embrace was all he needed to make his life complete.

Jake's total surrender always warmed Kohl's heart. He had taken in the animal because it was needy, felt good about caring for it because it was the right thing to do, and come to love it because it loved him unconditionally and asked little in return. He picked up Jake and laid him on Cara's bed, then lay down beside him. Jake soon was fast asleep.

Kohl was conflicted over recent happenings in his own life. It would be hard to explain why, but he believed that moving in with Cara would be a mistake. He regretted bringing his personal things from the old house. This signaled an intent to stay, of course, and she seemed pleased with what he'd done. How would she react when he told her he was going home?

He was grateful to Cara beyond words for her kindness and the affection she'd offered, and hurting her was the last thing in the world he wanted to do. But at the same time, he was afraid that the longer he stayed, the harder separation would be.

He was embarrassed by his own ignorance. Was a relationship like theirs common among women and men? How would his experiences differ if he had spent the last two decades living as a free man? He felt new resentment for his twenty years of incarceration—twenty years that had robbed him in ways he was only beginning to learn.

One thing that Kohl hated to admit to himself was his own cowardice. He always looked for an easy way out. In this case, the easy way was to leave now. If he stayed and made leaving hard, he might not have the courage to go through with it. He doubted that Cara planned to make a long-term commitment, and if she didn't a time would come when she'd ask him to move out. This would be the ultimate rejection. And it was rejection he feared most of all.

The longer he lay and considered these things, the more uncertain Kohl became about what to do. The deck was stacked against him. There would be pain now if he left and pain later if he stayed. Either way, it would be pain that he caused and he found this hardest of all to bear.

He left Jake lying on the bed and went to the kitchen. Impulsively, he began to rummage through drawers and open cabinet doors. He needed something that would ease the turmoil in his mind, silence the competing rages demanding his full attention, something that would gentle the stresses and help him avoid the explosion in his brain that he felt was inevitable unless he found relief.

Kohl knew about drugs. He had seen their effects on other prisoners, who always found ways to get them smuggled in. He'd seen strong men huddled in corners, weeping like babies, under their influence. He had seen peaceful men turn mean and mean men turn peaceful, and on one hot summer day he had seen the body of an inmate stretched out in the yard, dead from an overdose. Some said it was intentional; this man had chosen his own escape.

But why was he looking in the kitchen? If there were drugs in the trailer, they most likely would be in the bathroom.

Cara's bathroom was small, with fixtures crowded in tightly. A narrow medicine cabinet over the sink had a mirrored door that opened with only the slightest pull. A small prescription medicine bottle shared the top shelf with aspirin, toothpaste, and a box of flesh-toned adhesive bandages. The prescription bottle faced outward. Kohl could read the label in place, with no need to take the bottle from the shelf. The bottle contained generic hydrocodone. "For moderate pain," the label read, "Level 4 or 5."

Kohl was about to reach for the medicine bottle when he felt Jake's presence. He turned to look. Jake stood in the bathroom doorway, his tail wagging and excitement building in his eyes. The dog's love dance was about to begin.

Kohl suddenly felt guilty and embarrassed. How could he be so thoughtless as to take pills from Cara's medicine cabinet? Even if he told her later, he had been about to steal. His impetuous kitchen search was as vulgar as it was useless, and checking the contents of the medicine cabinet was an offensive act he was ashamed of. He slammed shut the medicine cabinet door and squatted on the floor. Jake rushed into his open arms.

"I apologize," Kohl said. "I'm sorry you saw that, Jake. You deserve a better human than me."

He picked up the dog and carried it back to the living room. Without loosening his hold, he sat down on the couch with Jake on his lap. Within minutes he could feel his tension beginning to ease.

"Doc Mueller taught us a way to deal with things when we got too up tight, and he wasn't too big on drugs," he said, speaking directly to Jake. "Doc was a counselor up at The Pines. He wasn't a doctor, but tried to act like one. He was a pretty good guy, though. I think you would have liked him."

Jake responded with a wide yawn.

"Well, sorry! I didn't mean to bore you. I thought since it's in the family you might like to hear what Doc told us, but I can see you're not too excited about all this. You can go back to sleep, then, and I'll work it out in my head. I'll be quiet, all right?"

Once Kohl had begun to take his advice seriously, Doc Mueller had helped him get through some particularly nasty days. In simplest terms, what the counselor taught was a form of self-analysis: mentally cataloging all the separate elements he could identify in a given problem area, ranking them in order of importance, and dealing with them in inverse order. The least-important factor should be the easiest to handle, the counselor said, and probably could be marked off the list quickly. Then deal with the next bottom issue, and then the next, and so on.

What Kohl had learned about his stress then suddenly seemed applicable now. New stresses had taken the place of old stresses, or in any case had been added to them. His new life was different and new stresses had germinated in different soil. But the answer Doc had offered had the same possibilities. His panic had no merit. He would face his demons standing tall, with Jake at his side should he need a crutch to lean on.

Kohl's mood improved as the morning wore on. He let Jake out for a second time and was wondering what there was to fix for lunch when he heard a car pull up in front of the trailer. Actually, the car proved to be George Spencer's truck.

"Danny Connor told me I might find you here," George Spencer said as Kohl greeted him at the door. "It's not like there's an emergency or anything, but I've been worrying about you in this cold and wondered if you could use my chainsaw and a ladder. You're going to need a lot more firewood than you can pick up off the ground, and one of those old oak trees needs to come down before it falls on the smokehouse. Not a big tree. If the two of us worked together we most likely could get it done in half a day."

Kohl was as surprised as he was pleased. "I didn't expect anything like this," he said. "You're the most considerate person I know. I'm really grateful."

"Unless you have something else planned, I'm ready to get to work on it right now. But that's up to you."

Kohl's response was an instant and unplanned decision. "Tell you what, Mr. Spencer, come in and sit for a few minutes while I get my things together and we can get back over to the old house and get started."

Jake followed the old man through the door. Kohl indicated the sofa as a place to sit and promised to be quick. Before gathering his things, he went to Cara's bedroom and scrawled a note on the back of the one she had left for him. He was uncertain what he should say, so he was brief and direct:

"Cara, Mr. Spencer came to help me with some important things over at the old house. He'll take Jake and me home and it's not likely we will get back over here tonight. I start work Monday, and I'll stay around long enough to be sure and see you at the PO. Thank you for everything. Kohl."

Twenty minutes later, he and Jake sat alongside George Spencer in the old man's ancient GMC pickup, on their way home. Kohl would have been content to ride in silence, but Mr. Spencer seemed eager to catch up on things. He had too much respect for the old man to not involve himself in friendly conversation.

"I sure hated it when your mom passed on," George Spencer was saying. "Where'd you say your sisters are at now?"

"One's in Arizona and one's in California," Kohl told him. "You and my mom were good friends, and she came to count on you for advice after Daddy died. Did she worry you to death sometimes with her questions? She didn't have anywhere else to turn."

"Lois and I loved your mom. She got to be like a sister to Lois. She deserved better than she had at the end, son. It would have been good to have you and your sisters around when she needed you most.

If it hadn't been for us, she probably would have died all by herself, there in that drafty old house with nobody else to care."

"Mr. Spencer, I would give my right arm—both arms and a leg—If I could go back and undo what I did. The years I spent in the pen were nothing next to the guilt and shame I feel for what I did to my mom and my sisters. It eats at me every day of my life. When I heard about Mom's passing, they had to put me on suicide watch. And it's probably a good thing they did. It'd be hard to hate anybody more than I hated myself."

George Spencer was slow to answer. "Life can be hard," he said after a moment of silence. "We all came into this world saddled with original sin. None of us deserves God's mercy, but in His goodness He sees fit to redeem us."

"I don't mean to be disrespectful," Kohl told him, "but it's not God I'm worried about right now. It's people. Fellow human beings. Even people I knew before, and thought were my friends. Wouldn't you think that over the years they might have got over some of their contempt for me? I want a chance to show them I can be a good person. Does that seem like too much to ask?"

George Spencer pursed his lips the way Kohl had seen him do many times. It was something he did when wanted to be especially careful in choosing his words.

"None of them has a right to sit in judgment," the old man said. "Maybe they haven't committed a sin as evident as yours, but they live their lives with sinful motives just like everyone else. It's only the day-to-day circumstances that set any one of us apart from any other. As far as giving you a second chance goes, we're still good people here. You were one of us once, and you know that. But I have to tell you, son, even where there's good people the rivers of mercy can run pretty shallow. Lots of people will allow that you served your time and paid a price, but don't expect much more than that."

NINE

WHILE KOHL CARRIED things into the house, George Spencer unloaded the ladder and chainsaw from the back of the truck and began a visual survey of the woodlot. Kohl fed Jake and put out food and water, then started a fire in the fireplace. Jake ate heartily and drank almost half the water in his pan, and when he'd finished he sat down and looked at Kohl as if waiting to see what came next.

"Just look at that dog!" Kohl said, feigning excitement. "Why, that must be Jake. And Jake's my buddy."

Jake went into his love dance. Kohl scuffed him on the head, took the dog's muzzle in his hands, and looked him directly in the eyes. "Stay in here where it's warm," he said. "I'll be working outside with Mr. Spencer. But I won't be far away, and I'll check in on you once in a while. Okay?"

He could feel Jake's eyes on him as he stood and went to the back door, but didn't look back. As he stepped out into the cold wind, he heard the first sounds of Mr. Spencer's chainsaw.

George Spencer already had cleared the undergrowth around the tree he said should be cut and had placed the ladder against the trunk at a level where he could reach the lower branches with the saw. "Stand back a ways 'til I get these limbs off," he called as Kohl approached. "Then we'll get this whole woodpile on the ground and begin working it up."

The old man's skill with the saw intrigued Kohl, who never had seen a chainsaw in use before. It looked dangerous. But Mr. Spencer used the tool like an artist. He systematically stripped branches from the trunk of the tree as high as his ladder would reach, then climbed down and quickly calculated the direction he wanted the tree to fall.

"Let's drag these limbs here on the east side over there where there's working room, and I'll fall it right this way," he said, motioning a projected path with his arm and hand. "Didn't you say you got a new axe? While I'm bringing her down, you can go get it. I'll be putting you to work before you know it!"

It took only a few minutes for the two men to drag the cut branches out of the way. Kohl went to the house to get his axe. He went in quietly, expecting Jake to be asleep, and his expectations were borne out. He stayed as quiet as he could as he got the axe and slipped back out. By the time he got to the woodlot George Spencer had the old oak tree almost ready to fall.

It was not a large tree, but when it came down there was a loud crash of branches breaking against the ground. Kohl tried not to show his astonishment at the violence of the fall; he assumed this was routine for George Spencer. But the old man obviously was excited, too, throwing up both hands as if signaling victory as soon as he had stopped the chainsaw and put it on the ground.

"She's bigger than I thought, Ernst," he called out. "Should be enough fireplace wood here to last you all winter, easy."

"You'd be a better judge of that than me," Kohl answered. "But you sure did a good job of getting it down. I wouldn't have had any idea how to go about it."

George Spencer looked past Kohl, toward the house. He frowned. "Don't look now, but we got company," he said in a low voice. But Kohl did turn and look. Deputy Scott Sobeski was about to join them. Neither of them said anything as he approached, waiting for him to speak first.

"I'd like a word with you, Kohl," Sobeski demanded. And turning to George Spencer, "Sir, if you'll excuse us, this is police business."

"There's nothing you're going to say that Mr. Spencer doesn't already know, Sobeski," Kohl said. "Whatever's on your mind, just spit it out!"

"Okay, then," Sobeski said. "We try to spare citizens embarrassment when we can, but if that's the way you want it that's the way we'll do it. I've got some questions about you and your dog, and you better have answers. You hear me?"

Kohl looked across at George Spencer, whose face showed no emotion. "Damn it, Sobeski," he said. "How come you have to pump everything up like there's a serial killer on the loose or something? Just ask me your questions and get it over with."

"Don't get smart with me, Kohl! I didn't get this badge out of a box of kid's breakfast cereal. You might as well get used to seeing my pretty face coming at you, because any time there's a crime anywhere in this county you're the first criminal I'm going to come calling on. You may think you're a pro now that you got in tight up there with the murderers and rapists and bank robbers and who knows what else, but I'm watching you like a hungry hawk watches a little field mouse. You're not going to get away with anything in my county."

George Spencer took a step forward. "Young man," he said to Sobeski, "I'm one of the citizens who pays your salary and I'm not intimidated by your damned badge. There's no reason to harass anybody the way you just did. If you have questions for my friend and neighbor here, ask them in a polite, professional way and get on with it."

Sobeski turned awkwardly to face his accuser, his reddening face distorted with an expression that was somewhere between disbelief and anger. "Sir," he said, "harassment is not the way we work in the sheriff's department, and it's not the way I operate personally. We are here to protect the citizens of this county, people like you. But when a crime happens, we pursue the case vigorously. That's what I'm trained to do."

He turned back to face Kohl. "As I was saying, I have some questions about that dog you had. Still got it?" He had lowered his voice to a less demanding level.

"Yes."

"I believe you said it's a stray. Did you make any effort to find the owner?"

"No."

"And the dog came to your door?"

"Yes. I think I told you that."

"Somebody out on this side of the county says their collie dog was stolen recently, Kohl." Sobeski's voice had risen again. "I don't suppose that dog of yours happens to be a collie?"

Kohl had a hard time not laughing. "You saw him. Did you see any collie in him? Or do you even know what a collie looks like?" As soon as he'd said those words, he knew this was a mistake. Sobeski was not one to take questions like this lightly. He had not intended to antagonize the deputy, in fact would have leaned over backward not to had he been thinking before he spoke.

"Dammit, Kohl," Sobeski roared, "I ask the questions. You answer them. Is that dog a collie or not? And you'd better not lie to me! I can take that dog in for evidence if I have to. I'm giving you a break here—something that's against my better judgment to begin with. Now I'll ask you one more time: Is the damned dog a collie? Yes or no!"

"No, sir. It's a mixed breed, and I'd say there's no visible collie in him. Wouldn't you agree, Mr. Spencer?"

George Spencer had stood by quietly since his earlier outburst. He said firmly, "Yes, I agree. I know dogs as well as anybody and I'd say there's no collie in that one. Not a single ounce."

Deputy Scott Sobeski suddenly seemed to be in a hurry. "Gentlemen, I'm still the chief investigator on this case. We don't stand by idly when somebody's dog gets stolen. I hope I don't have to come back on this one, but I'm watching you, Kohl." And directly to the old man, "Have a good day, sir."

He walked rapidly back the way he'd come.

"I think we can see that Deputy Sobeski's not the brains in the sheriff's department," Kohl said to George Spencer. "But I understand he can be dangerous. I didn't intend to make him mad."

"And I probably didn't do you any favors by talking back to him the way I did. I'm sorry, son. His arrogance just got to me."

"Mr. Spencer, hearing you jump on that cocky little rooster was worth a million dollars. Nothing's going to make him any worse. And just thinking about the look on his face when you finished with him will keep me laughing for a long time to come."

George Spencer slapped him on the shoulder and laughed. "Well, then I'm glad I did it," he said. "It felt good to me, too. Now let's get back to work and get some firewood cut. Tonight's going to be another cold one."

———————

By the time it got too dark to work, they had half the branches of the felled oak tree cut into lengths appropriate for burning in the fireplace. They had much of this stacked neatly just outside the kitchen door. George Spencer appeared to be well pleased with what they'd accomplished, and promised to get back from time to time with his chainsaw and work up the rest. He said he would cut the trunk into sections which they would split into fire logs with wedges and a sledge hammer.

"Before I leave, Ernst, I have something for you," he said, standing next to his truck. "Here. This is still plenty cold."

He lifted a small ice chest from the back of the truck and set it on the ground.

"I took you a couple of beef steaks and a chicken out of the deep freeze," he said. "I've got more than I need, and I thought maybe you could use them. I suppose you've got cooking pans and all that?"

Kohl was embarrassed to have to tell him how little he had to work with, including no gas connection for the kitchen range. "But I can cook these over the fireplace," he added quickly. "Nothing better than a steak cooked over an open flame. Thank you, Mr. Spencer. I'll get all this stuff taken care of as soon as I can. First thing is, I have to find out where to go."

George Spencer fixed his eyes on the younger man in what could only be described as a glare. "You mean you don't have utilities yet? Why didn't you tell me? Number one, I'd have made you come and stay with me. And number two, I'd have helped get that done. You're still welcome to come home with me if you want, but either way I'll go into town tomorrow and take care of all that for you. Damn, boy, you can't hardly get by without electricity. And how about a mailbox? I didn't see one out there by the road. You'll have to have an address for them to send the bills to. I'll go by the post office and work that out while I'm at it. And I'll bring you a mailbox."

Kohl was too overwhelmed to protest. Anyway, when Mr. Spencer made up his mind to do something, all the bears in the North Woods couldn't stop him. This simply would be added to the list of good things that had happened to him on this day, and for all of them he was grateful.

"One more thing," George Spencer said. "You need music. I'll see if I can't find you an inexpensive little radio."

"Well, sure. That would be great. But I'll bet they don't play much U2 anymore."

"Don't bet on it, lad. Nowadays you can find just about anything you want on the radio. Anyway, I'll be in touch."

After the old man left, Kohl set the ice chest just outside the kitchen door. Given the low air temperature, nothing would thaw and the food would be safe—such as was left. He took out one of the steaks and the chicken and cooked them over the open flames in the fireplace. Jake got most of the chicken and a generous portion of the steak.

"You got any collie in you, Jake?" he teased. "I sure don't see it if you do!"

Jake went into his love dance.

"Just look at that dog!" Kohl said, scuffing Jake's head. "Jake's my buddy! And that makes old Kohl the luckiest man in the world."

The day's work had left Kohl dead tired, and the steak had left him with a full stomach. He brought a couple of the oak fire logs close and lay down beside Jake on the mattress on the floor. Cara would be going to bed now, too. Could he have shared her bed only last night? It already seemed as if it had happened much longer ago—if it happened at all. He lay awake briefly reliving in his senses the passion the two had shared. He could feel the warmth and softness of her body, his own breathlessness when they coupled as one. He had given himself completely over to an encore of the pleasures of making love to Cara when he fell fast asleep.

In his dreams, though, it was Angie who lay beside him. Their night was complex and exciting. They sat close together on the leather-covered sofa in her house, talking about things they knew little about. Then there were soft kisses. And they talked more and listened to music. More soft kisses became passionate kisses. He felt for her breast and she did not resist. And they lay body-to-body, unclothed, thrilled by exploring hands and more soft kisses and his mouth on her breasts and more passionate kisses and they were overtaken by mutual desire. In the dreams he made love to Angie just as he had made love to Cara and his pent-up yearning was fulfilled.

TEN

ERNST KOHL HAD come of age in a setting where standards were rigid and almost universally accepted. He did not remember either of his grandfathers, but his father had told him and his sisters many times how their Grandfather Kohl made his way from Germany to the United States between world wars with nothing except the clothes on his back "and his good word."

His family held no monopoly on the respect for truth, of course. Most of those in the social circles through which they moved took for granted the integrity of their friends and neighbors. Kohl would trust the word of men like George Spencer even if his life hung in the balance.

His mother also had preached the gospel of truth and honor above all else, and had led her children to believe that telling a lie would be the ultimate dishonor through which they could sully their father's memory. "Once you tell a lie," she said, "you are a liar, and once you are a liar nobody will ever trust you again." As a boy he had come to believe that lying surely must be a far more serious transgression than almost anything else short of murder.

Ada and Hannah had taken her words to heart the same as he had, and more than once he'd lain on the closet floor and listened to their condemnation of one girlfriend or another for being dishonest. It seemed that the lies almost always involved relationships with boys, and by coincidence the boys almost always were ones his sisters had crushes on.

It wasn't until he took up residence at The Pines Correctional Center that Kohl came to fully understand the extent to which this was a standard commonly disregarded by much of society. There were men within those fences who had no more respect for honesty than Jake had for fancy clothes. Truth would never be allowed to stand between them and whatever it was they wanted.

But somebody else's shortcomings could never be used as an excuse for his own failures, and even to this day he felt almost as much guilt and shame over the lies he'd told about events that awful day twenty years ago as he did for the terrible act he was guilty of. The Kohl moral code did not allow for extenuating circumstances like those he faced that night. And it was easy to rationalize that the act was not intended, whereas he'd had a choice whether to lie or tell the truth.

Jake was his family now. Jake was honest to the core. Jake would never lie to him or deliberately mislead him because of envy or greed, and Jake would never tell him one thing to his face and say otherwise behind his back. Jake's love and loyalty were strong enough to endure through thick and thin. This is what Kohl believed, and he had infinite confidence in his conviction.

As usually happened when it came to Jake, Kohl's thoughts soon developed into words. And as usual, when he talked Jake offered his full attention.

"You're superior to the human race in a lot of ways," Kohl said, looking straight into the dog's eyes. "You wouldn't know how to lie if you wanted to. I don't mean lie down, I mean tell a lie. You know, say something that's not true."

Jake's ears stood up. The eagerness in his eyes said he wanted to hear more.

"You and me never argue, Jake. That's unusual for family. Come here and let me give you some noggin knuckles."

Jake came to him, as if he had understood Kohl's words. Kohl grabbed him under the chin and scuffed his head, knuckles down. Jake started his love dance, but stopped suddenly and stood perfectly still, rigid as a statue. Then a throaty growl.

George Spencer was at the back door. Kohl opened the door and Jake relaxed.

"I picked up a few things you're going to need," the old man said, not waiting for greetings from Kohl and not offering any himself. "Little stuff, you know, like light bulbs. They ought to have your power turned on by the end of the week. You'll get gas at the same time, and you might even get water today. There's a little radio in there, too, for when you get power to plug it into. And I brought you some clothes—some of my perfectly good things that I can't wear anymore. They ought to fit you and I thought you could use them."

He carried a large bag marked "Baum Farm Supply" in one hand and what looked like a laundry bag in the other.

Kohl shook his head. "What can I say, Mr. Spencer? You've been awful good to me. You know there's no way I can ever pay you back."

George Spencer's face flushed, ever so slightly. "Ernst," he said, "your bill's already been taken care of. Your dad and mom, especially your mom, did more for Lois and me than I could repay in two lifetimes. I can tell you, your dad was one of the best men I've ever known and your mom, well, your mom was a saint. Lois loved her like a sister."

Jake walked a tight circle around Kohl's legs, then offered his head to the other man to see if he could get more scuffing. He did.

"I'm beginning to think real highly of your dog," George Spencer said. "And excuse me for bringing up somebody I don't hold in such high regard, but do you suppose that deputy's found out the difference between your dog here and a collie yet? What's his name? I knew it when I started this and now I can't think of it!"

"Deputy Scott Sobeski! I think he wanted me to tattoo it on my hand or something."

"Oh, yes. Scott Sobeski, lawman! He would be disappointed to know I forgot his name. Heard from him lately?"

Kohl made a noise somewhere between a grunt and a groan. "No, but I'm afraid to say so. Little Robocop might show up at the front door any time now."

"We can sure hope he doesn't. But by the way, I went to the agency that handled this place as rental property to get a key, and they couldn't find one. Just to be safe, I got new locks for both doors and I've got a glass for that window there, on the truck. Kind of surprised I remembered the glass, except it was so blasted cold out there this morning. You know how the furnace and water pump and all that works?"

"I guess not. I didn't even remember there was a water pump, and the furnace was put in after I left. Lots of changes in twenty years."

"All in good time, Ernst, all in good time. And you need to know that the furnace won't heat the downstairs real well. You'll still need to use the fireplace. Look, I've got to go, but I'll get back when they come to hook things up. They're supposed to call me. I'll glaze that window then, too. You good for now?"

Kohl smiled what he thought might be his most genuine smile since he walked through the gates leaving The Pines. "Yes, sir," he answered. "I'm a lot better off now than I was yesterday, too. I can't ever thank you—"

George Spencer waved off his comment and turned to the door. When he opened it a gust of frigid air rushed in. "Oughtn't to be this cold yet," he said. "Looks like it may be a long winter."

Kohl closed the door behind him, then turned to Jake. "You and me got some work to do," he said. "For starters, let's put in some light bulbs. And you know what? It's time you see the upstairs. There's a lot more to this place than you know!"

He took a carton of light bulbs from one of the bags George Spencer had brought, and Jake trotted beside him as he walked toward the stairs. After picking up one of his mother's old dinette chairs to stand on, he went up a half-dozen steps and stopped and looked back. Jake sat on the floor looking up but not moving.

"Come on, boy," he said. "I wouldn't let you try something that might be dangerous, would I? You can do it. Just follow me."

He turned back toward the top of the stairs and very deliberately, one step at a time, climbed on up to the second-floor landing. Jake scampered up behind him.

They started with the bathroom, then went into the first of three bedrooms. Its lighting fixture hung from the ceiling and Kohl, standing on the chair, had to stretch to reach it. There was no bulb in the fixture. He quickly screwed in a new one and stepped down.

"We'll have this place all lit up in no time," he said casually, continuing his running, one-way conversation with Jake. "And when we get the furnace working, this will be the warmest room in the house. Probably be where we hang out. But don't worry, you'll get used to the stairs. They're good exercise, too. Keep you from getting fat."

Kohl sat down in the chair. Jake lay down and stretched out at his feet.

This had been his mother's room. Surely there had been times when she wanted to escape to this place, hidden away behind these four walls, to find the exquisite peace and quiet that comes only with solitude. But her door always was open to him and his sisters. No matter the day or the hour, she assured them, and no matter what they wanted to talk about.

After the death of their father, there were many nights when he and his sisters congregated in this room after supper to be with her. In his mind's eye he could see her pretty face, barely beginning to age, and the clear blue eyes and reddish-brown hair, touched here and there with gray. The simple comfort of her presence was enough. Sometimes all three spent the night with her, Ada and Hannah lying at her side and young Ernst lying across the foot of the bed.

There had been occasions when he wanted and needed to talk but was too embarrassed to ask her about things that bothered him. These most often involved changes brought on by puberty—a word he'd never heard—both in himself and his sisters. He knew from overheard conversations that the girls felt free to go to her with their questions, and that she always did her best to give them straight answers. But his information came from the older boys at school, and his information was not always correct.

"You would have liked her, Jake," he said. "My mother, I mean. She would have liked you, too, no doubt about that. You're a real good boy and she was a real good woman. I was the only boy she had and I wasn't nearly as good as you!"

Jake sat up and looked him in the eyes. Kohl scuffed his head and went on talking.

"My mother was a saint, just like Mr. Spencer said. Wasn't any sacrifice she wouldn't make for us, you know what I'm saying? She'd have gone without food if she had to so we could eat. This was her room, did I say? I did an awful thing to her, Jake. I hurt her so much I know she never got over it. She deserved a lot better son than me."

When Kohl stopped talking, Jake lay down again, but this time across his feet. Kohl stooped in his chair to stroke the dog's back. He had tears in his eyes.

"Like Mr. Spencer said, she shouldn't have been here all by herself in her last years. She could have died all alone in this old house, Jake. She must have felt like we deserted her. And she did all she could for us . . . everything she could have done, Jake."

Kohl began to sob softly. When he spoke again his voice was husky and broken. "They wouldn't let me come. I couldn't even come to her funeral. But maybe that was best, Jake. Nobody wanted to see me. She was such a good person. So good. Like Mr. Spencer said, she was a saint. And I should have told her the truth, Jake. We were protecting Angie, but I hurt my mother so much. I should have told her the truth."

For the next hour, he sat silently in his mother's old dinette chair in the middle of his mother's room. Jake lay at his feet but did not sleep.

Kohl had few vivid memories of his father. There was a general image: tall and thin—the body build his son inherited—with a thick shock of black hair, soft gray eyes, and a seemingly permanent smile. He kept a positive attitude but could be quite passionate about things he thought were important. One of these was the inherent equality of all people and parallel disdain for oppression in any form. Kohl supposed this came from his German background and was rooted in family experiences, as passed down by Kohl's grandfather, but he did not recall any specific discussion of the subject.

One thing his father did not feel strongly about—or perhaps more accurately, felt strongly about in a negative way—was farming. He always said he was not cut out to be a farmer, and at the first good opportunity sold the large Kohl family farm inherited from Grandfather Kohl and took a job in town with the John Deere tractor and implement dealer. Money from the land sale was a windfall. He used a small portion of it to buy a substantial life insurance policy on himself and put the rest into an interest-paying trust that turned out to be enough to support the family after his death so that Kohl's mother never had to work.

His father's death was attributed to an uncomplicated heart attack. Kohl's mother always believed that he knew he was at risk and carefully planned for his family's welfare. She maintained that this was true testament to her husband's sterling character.

Most of what Kohl remembered about his father was a residue of special events that brought the family together. Christmases, Thanksgiving dinners, his own and his sisters' birthdays. And most prominent among these were short, happy family trips, especially a couple taken on the Fourth of July. His father insisted that "our nation's birthday" be celebrated, and his preferred way to celebrate was to pack everyone in a car and go to someplace they'd never been before for a picnic.

Kohl's mother would prepare a feast, carefully packed in two large baskets and a cold-pack with lots of ice, lemonade, and tea. Once at the site selected, the young Kohl and his father would spread a canvas tarp on the ground and then an old quilt on top of that. His mother and sisters would unpack the food and drink and for the next hour everyone enjoyed the picnic meal and each other's company.

His father always managed to find a different way home. Everyone got to see more sights this way, he said. And on this holiday it was important for the children to "see America." America, in the Kohl family's small world, consisted entirely of interesting and not too-distant spots in Michigan.

He remembered his father and mother talking about taking a longer trip "sometime," maybe going to the nation's capital or to New England. It would be when the kids were older, and could better appreciate what they saw. But his father's sudden death left that dream unfulfilled.

The one trip Kohl remembered best was the last one, the year his father died. The family's Independence Day outing took them to Frankenmuth. After their picnic in a beautiful park, his father drove them around the community to see the Bavarian-style architecture for which the town was famous.

"This could be your Grandfather Kohl's home town in the old country," he told the kids. He said he hoped to be able to go to Germany one day himself, to see where generations of Kohls came from.

Memories of that day no longer were happy ones. Kohl felt sad that his father never had an opportunity to live that particular dream. Life could be very unfair.

ELEVEN

THE HOT SHOWER struck Kohl as the most luxurious experience he ever could ask for. He stood under the stream of water and let the heat relax tense muscles and permeate his body. The space between the shower curtain and the wall was a block of steam, which merely added to his euphoria. He would have been content to stay in this spot all day. After a time, though, he began to feel burned by the water and reluctantly decided he needed to get out.

George Spencer's work had paid off. The old house now had electricity, gas, and running water. There was a mailbox in front of the house with the name E. Kohl on it, and he had the new clothes his elderly neighbor had brought him, along with some towels and bed linens. He had not—and would not—put sheets on the dirty mattress he and Jake slept on, but with luck he'd soon have a bed in his mother's room and the place would begin taking on some semblance of a lived-in home.

When he was dry and dressed, he hurried downstairs to the kitchen. Jake sat in the middle of the room, watching through the window in fascination as George Spencer worked on the outside, putting in new glass. He was so caught up in this that he appeared not to notice that Kohl was coming.

"Should a been in the shower with me, Jake," he called out to the dog. "First time I've been really warm since my dog was just a pup. Oh, wait. That would be you, and you're still just a pup."

Jake turned and ran to him and promptly went into his love dance.

"Who's the smartest, toughest dog there ever was?" Kohl sang out. "Why, it's Jake. Look at the way his ears stand up when I speak! Jake's my buddy!"

George Spencer was just finishing the repairs to the broken window, and soon was inside with them. "Good thing I was working on the south side of the house," he said. "Wind out there's right off the North Pole this morning. Your shower work good, Ernst?"

"Mr. Spencer, that was the best shower any human being ever had! I never knew hot water could feel so good."

"Well, you know what they say about cleanliness, son. Before you know it we'll have you down right godly. You say you're going to work down at the Purple Onion next week?"

"Yes, sir, I am."

"I believe it was Seneca who said the evils of idleness can be shaken off by hard work. Keeps you out of trouble, in other words."

"And it will be damned—sorry, Mr. Spencer—darned good to get on a payroll."

The old man laughed heartily, something Kohl had seldom heard. "I'm not a prude, Ernst," he said. "It's not something I'm especially proud of, but I can cuss with the best of 'em when something goes wrong. Lois used to get onto me sometimes for my foul language."

"I don't think I ever heard you cuss, or say a bad word of any kind. And I remember a few things going wrong when we were out there picking cherries."

"I tried to hold my temper when there were young people around."

The warm comfort Kohl still felt from the shower was magnified by this visit with George Spencer. More than any other person still alive, Mr. Spencer represented to him the generation of his father and mother, a generation otherwise lost to him forever. Listening to the old man talk, he could almost imagine that his mother was busy putting breakfast on the table or even that his father was bringing in wood for the fireplace.

His earlier comprehension that it took people to make a home was being borne out, and George Spencer was high on his list of people who mattered. With Jake lying at his feet and Mr. Spencer talking about old times, it was almost as if he were back in the home he'd left behind when he was taken in handcuffs and shackles twenty years ago.

"Come back over to the house with me and have some breakfast," George Spencer said. "And bring that vicious watch dog, too. Jake and I are getting to be pretty good friends."

Kohl accepted the invitation eagerly. Fifteen minutes later the two men and the dog were in the Spencer house. Kohl walked about, renewing memories of a home he'd spent many hours in during his youth. When he got to the kitchen, Mr. Spencer was making a breakfast of steak and eggs. The coffee already was hot. Jake chewed contentedly on a strip of rawhide and Kohl sat at the table watching his old friend at work over the stove and taking in the pleasures of a functioning farm-house kitchen.

"I'd forgot how many books you have," he said to the old man. "Have you really read them all?"

"Probably not," George Spencer said. "Life's not fair, you know. Now that I have lots of time to read, these tired old eyes don't stand up to too much of it."

"I did more reading in The Pines than I ever had before. It helped pass the time."

"Time is something I am beginning to treasure, Ernst. I guess you talked to Jack Gengler?"

"Yes, sir, I did."

"You know him before?"

"No, sir, I didn't. He struck me as a nice enough guy, and the people who work at the grill seem to think he's okay. Do you know him?"

George Spencer waited until he'd finished turning steaks and eggs in two frying pans on the stove before he answered. "Oh, yes," he said then, "I've known Jack for years. Never saw anything but good in him. He's been the manager of that little grill for about as long as I remember."

"You ever come over there? To eat, I mean."

"Lois and I used to go over there for breakfast once in a while, just for something different. I've not been back since I lost her."

Kohl wasn't sure how to respond. He did not want to turn this happy occasion into a mournful remembrance service. His slowness to answer led the other man to go on speaking.

"Jack is the manager," he said, "but he doesn't own the place. A man I don't know, named Rasmusan, I think, owns the Purple Onion and the old Dairy Queen where you used to work and two or three other places in town. Another case of big money being in control. But this stuff is about ready, now. Let's have breakfast."

The old man carried a skillet to the table and scooped a mound of scrambled eggs onto each of their plates, and went back and got the steaks and repeated the routine. He poured more coffee, then pulled a chair out from the table opposite Kohl and sat down to eat.

Steak and eggs was a breakfast combination Kohl never had had before. It was a matter of only a few seconds until he found that he'd been missing a treat. "I have to tell you," he said, "this has to be the best breakfast I've ever had. I always thought you only got a steak for dinner."

"Lois introduced me to it. I'd never had it before, either. She was a wonderful cook. Now that I'm all by myself, I hardly bother to cook. Not very good at it, anyway."

"She was always one of my favorite people," Kohl said. "Even when I was just a little kid she always treated me with respect. You know, like she credited me with some good sense even if I wasn't a grownup. I've never forgot that."

George Spencer was intent on carving the meat on his plate into bite-size pieces. He didn't say anything until he had finished. After he put down his knife, he looked Kohl directly in the eyes. "Ernst," he said, "God has been very generous to me. When you come to the end of your life, you don't look back on the material things you accumulated. You look back on the people you loved who loved you back. You may know, I went to a seminary and studied theology. I wanted to be a pastor—"

"You would have made a great one," Kohl interrupted.

"Be that as it may. Things don't always work out the way we expect them to. Anyway, I took a seminar in marriage counseling. They taught us that there are three great loves in a man's life, Ernst: his first love, his perfect love, and his last love. If he's fortunate, as I was, these are all the same. Lois was my soulmate, my perfect love. And she was my childhood sweetheart. As I said, God was very generous to me."

This time, it was Jake who interrupted. Evidently deciding that real steak smelled a lot better than his rawhide chew, he approached Kohl with a soft whine. When that didn't get immediate action, the whine turned into a bark. Jake was not timid when it came to seeking attention.

"Okay, fellow, you can have a bite," Kohl said. He picked up a piece of steak with his fingers and held it out to the dog. Jake took it in his mouth gently, as if he were afraid it might be breakable.

George Spencer held up a hand, pretending a formal request for permission to speak. "I need to amend an earlier statement," he announced. "With consent of my peers, of course."

The charade was wasted on Kohl, who had no clue what the joke was. But he sensed that he was supposed to respond, so he said, "Yes, of course."

"Thank you, my good man," George Spencer said, maintaining an appropriate level of formality. "I believe I said you look back on the *people* you love, who love you back. My amendment would change this to *all those* you love. We would never want to overlook faithful companions like Jake, here. Would you not agree?"

"Sir, I agree wholeheartedly," Kohl said, falling into line with the old man's little game. "Jake is more than just family, too. It may not be visible to you, sir, but Jake and I are joined at the heart."

TWELVE

WHEN KOHL RODE up to the Purple Onion at ten o'clock Monday night, he was a bundle of nerves. He hadn't seen Cara since the night he shared her bed. He felt guilty for running out on her the way he did, knowing she expected him to be there when she got home that day. She wouldn't be at the grill this late, but he had promised in his note to wait for her in the morning. He had no notion what her reaction might be.

He hadn't intended to hurt Cara. How could he? To be with her—to sleep in her bed—had been far more than he would have dared even to hope for. But then he'd given in to his own insecurity, let it take control. In his heart he longed to stay, but didn't. How could he have been so foolish? She had given him bliss and he'd rejected it in favor of what—empty dreams of Angie? He was embarrassed by his own inanity.

He had wanted desperately to go back to Cara's place the next day and be waiting for her when she got home from the Purple Onion. But there had been Jake to care for, the potential need for him to be at the old house should Mr. Spencer succeed in arranging utility connections quickly, such cleaning up as he could manage, and any number of other rationalizations. The truth was, he was afraid. Cara would be justified in rejecting him on sight.

So far as his new job was concerned, Kohl wasn't overly confident that there really was work for him to do. Even with his limited experience, he had developed a strong and binding work ethic. He'd hired out as a farm hand as a teenager, usually doing labor-intensive jobs like picking cherries. His later job at the Dairy Queen was so important to him that he worried constantly about being late or not performing up to expected standards. And in his longest-held job, working in prison industries, punctuality and keeping his nose to the grindstone were essential if he was to hang on to a privilege not all prisoners were granted.

But he had been thinking back to the morning Danny Connor showed up at the old house and said he could work at the grill if he wanted to. Danny hadn't said they needed to replace somebody, or business had gotten better and they needed more help, nor offered any other reason why this position suddenly existed. He had said, simply, that Jack Gengler had approved his hiring, "if you need a job." More than anything else, this looked like an act of charity.

He had hoped to bring up the subject with George Spencer when the two of them were at work in the woodlot. Most of his farm labor had been in the hire of Mr. Spencer, and it was during those long working days that he had come to respect Mr. Spencer's wisdom and admire his ability to explain complex ideas in simple ways the young Kohl could understand. And Mr. Spencer had been adamant that charity ought to begin at home. Whether it was his prized cherries or any other commodity he produced, he always found ways to share his abundance with the less fortunate.

But did any of this really matter? He needed the money. If his new job was a handout from Danny Connor and Jack Gengler, he'd accept it with gratitude. And work hard to make sure they had no regrets.

Kohl went in and looked about the dining area, assessing the level of business. There were only three men in the room and he took all of them to be truck drivers. Two of them sat together in a booth near the front, and the third sat alone at the counter in back. Danny Connor was busy tending to something on the hot griddle.

As Kohl approached, Danny acknowledged him without looking up. "I'll be with you in a minute. Glad you came."

Kohl took a seat at the counter, next to the truck driver. The man barely glanced his way.

"Getting cold out there," Kohl said, hoping to strike up a conversation.

"Hell, yes," the man responded. "It's winter. Winter's cold."

This brought Danny Connor into the game. "You don't sound too chipper tonight, Jimbo," he said. "Kohl, meet Jim Endicott—

'Full-throttle Jimbo' in the elite trucking circles. Jimbo, Kohl here's a high school classmate of mine."

Jim Endicott turned to Kohl and thrust out a hand. "Glad to meet you," he said. "I have to warn you, though, that being a friend of this fellow's no great recommendation."

"I don't even know him," Kohl said, wanting to carry on the give-and-take spirit. "Glad to meet you, too. Are you a regular at this fine dining establishment?"

Before Jim Endicott could answer, Danny jumped back in. "Jim runs an open route that covers all of Michigan except the UP. He won't admit it, but I guarantee you he goes a hundred miles out of his way at least once a week just to get his hands on a cup of our notorious coffee. Isn't that right, Jimbo?"

The driver, a short, squatty man Kohl guessed to be in his fifties, threw up his hands. "Guilty!" he declared. "I hate to admit it, because Danny's already famous all over the state and don't need his ego salved. But like they used to say in the old cigarette ads, or maybe it was beer, I'd walk ten feet for a cup of Danny Connor's coffee."

The facetious chatter had brightened Kohl's spirit. He was beginning to feel good simply being among men who could enjoy themselves through nothing more than trying to outdo each other in witty conversation. He had experienced this occasionally in prison, but usually the conversation was mean and vulgar rather than witty.

"Want some coffee, Kohl?" Danny Connor asked. "You got plenty of time, 'cause I can't get loose from here to get you started just now. Don't worry, though, I already put you on the clock."

Kohl was happy to get something hot. And the lack of pressure to get him into an apron or whatever his work garb was led him to relax a bit.

"So you work here?" Jim Endicott asked.

"I'm supposed to. I'm just now checking in for the first time."

"Well, I got some advice for you. Get in tight with that gypsy waitress—Carla or something like that. I can tell you there's more than one trucker who stops in here just hoping to get her to stick a finger in his coffee."

Kohl turned toward Danny Connor, hoping for some word disavowing the trucker's offensive insinuation. Danny never looked up.

"Maybe you mean Cara," he said to Jim Endicott, his tone unwittingly cold. "I know her, if that's who you're talking about."

He was stunned by what he had just heard and he wanted this conversation to go no further. He was afraid to hear more. Of course Cara was popular with the customers. Given his own physical attraction to her, how could it never have occurred to him that she might have similar appeal to any other man who stopped by the Purple Onion?

"Well, whatever," Jim Endicott said. "I've got to get it back in gear. Hey, Danny, keep the coffee hot. I'll be back before you know I'm gone." With this, he slid from the stool beside Kohl and walked briskly toward the front door.

"Hell, he didn't even give me time to answer him," Danny Connor said over his shoulder. "But that's Jimbo. When he's ready to move, he moves. Give me about two more minutes, Kohl, and I'll see if I can get you in the harness and ready to go to work."

Kohl did not reply. He was not aware that Danny had spoken to him. His mind was back in The Pines Correctional Center.

David Murray McKenzie's bitterness toward women, his firm conviction that "none of them is any damned good," had just flared through Kohl's consciousness like a bolt of lightning from a clear blue sky. McKenzie, the lifer with no possibility of parole, the man who claimed to have made his peace with God and accepted his fate without a plea for mercy—David Murray McKenzie was in prison for murdering his wife. It was the jolting circumstances that led to this brutal act that Kohl thought about now.

"So let's go on back here and I'll get you started," Danny Connor was saying. And when he got no response: "Kohl? Ready to go to work?"

This time, Kohl heard. He followed Danny to the cramped adjacent cold-room where the grill's supplies were stored and where clean dishware was loaded on racks and dirty dishes were stacked in a deep, stainless steel double sink along the wall. There was no dishwashing machine; the work here was all done by hand.

"When we have waitresses, they pick up the dirty dishes and bring 'em back here to the sink," Danny Connor said. "I do it at night. Most of the time we're not that busy in the late hours. If you're not kept busy at the sink, I'll probably ask you to pick up dishes. That sound okay?"

"Sure, Danny. Whatever you need me to do. By the way, who does this during the daytime?"

"There's four or five women. Jack keeps the schedule and rotates them, is the way I understand it."

There was a stack of dishes and silverware in the sink. Danny showed Kohl where supplies were kept and urged him to use water as hot as he could stand and plenty of soap. They shared a joke about his lack of experience and need for formal training in dishwashing, then Danny went back to the griddle and Kohl was left alone with his work and his thoughts. David Murray McKenzie was still on his mind.

McKenzie still was a relatively young man, probably in his late forties. Although Kohl had come to know him well, he couldn't remember if he ever knew how long the one-time professional hockey player already had served. What he did know was that McKenzie was serving two life sentences with no possibility of parole.

Making friends in any penal institution would be challenging, Kohl assumed, given the general level of suspicion and mistrust. And for him, there was a formidable amount of added baggage that made the challenge infinitely tougher. He arrived at The Pines a good deal younger than the average offender housed in the institution, shy, and terribly naïve. There was no preparation for the ordeal ahead. He had never been away from home before he was jailed, he'd never experienced regimentation of any kind, and his short life to this point had been spent in a quiet and loving family. When he first set foot on the prison grounds he was so scared he soiled his pants.

His new and terrifying surroundings left him lying awake at night, afraid to sleep until total exhaustion took control and discombobulated his dreams into a mix of beauty and revulsion. Either way, they always centered on Angie and played out in his subconscious like streaming music themes without structure. Memories, moonlit nights, speaking of love, love is forever, love fresh as the morning dew, desires ungratified, one in spirit, sorry, sorry, Angie's eyes, solitary, sorry Angie, together, together, together forever, forgive me Angie, touching, loving and being loved, world apart, love deeper than the sea, Angie's smile, splendor, together forever and forever, no one without the other, Angie's touch, Angie's kisses, love, together forever, together forever.

David Murray McKenzie spotted him one day, standing beneath the gym bars in the yard trying to be invisible. Kohl still recalled his first words: "You look like a mouse in a room full of cats. It takes a while, but you'll get used to it."

He should have been suspicious. This man wanted something. But there had been something about McKenzie that had the feel of trusted friendship from the very beginning. It may have been the soft-spoken, gentle manner, or maybe Kohl had been so desperate for human warmth that he would have been easily taken in. Either way, he looked back on that day now as the most lucky one in his years at The Pines. McKenzie had taken him under a wing like a mother goose and never asked anything in return.

Fortunately, Kohl had been too timorous to ask his new friend and protector anything about his past. Fortunate because, as he learned eventually, it was an unwritten rule among offenders that you never ask another man why he's there. Let him tell you on his own terms. And even though McKenzie had manifested a deep-seated antagonism toward women, Kohl had been stunned when he first heard that this placid man's crime was the vicious murder of his own wife.

On a warm summer night, McKenzie had decided to put an end to the anguish and humiliation of lying nearly helpless in his bed and listening to his wife have sex with another man in an adjacent room. He had endured physical pain beyond what few people ever would experience—an ascending ladder of open-spine surgeries to repair the repeated damage from brutal contact on the ice. After his third operation, he came home from the hospital facing an extended period of bed-fast recuperation. But the physical pain, he told the young Kohl after finally opening up about his past, was nothing compared to the torture of his wife's behavior.

"Night after night," he said, his bitterness evident in the expression of his words, "she'd go out to a bar and bring back some guy to make out with. Right outside my door. She took some kind of sadistic pleasure in knowing I could hear them. One night I just couldn't take it anymore."

In a fit of rage, McKenzie had dragged himself out of bed, picked up a heavy object—he didn't remember what it was—and gone to the other room and bludgeoned his wife to death. He hit the man, also, and knocked him unconscious. Then he called the police. The man died later in the hospital so he was charged with double murder. He demanded that his court-appointed attorney launch no serious defense, and was convicted by a jury that deliberated less than an hour.

Kohl had sensed that his fellow prisoner felt no remorse, and nothing he was told had differed from this. He struggled with the comparisons between his own crime and McKenzie's. Both men had acted out of fits of passion, but the similarities ended there. Unlike his friend, Kohl had intended no harm and still suffered endless pangs of guilt and shame for what he did.

He wanted easy answers, but there were none. Of course the failure of one man's wife was not a reflection on all wives, and certainly not on all women. Like his mother used to say, "Ernst, you can't tar everybody with the same broad brush." But he never could have imagined that things with Angie might turn out the way they did, either. He was beginning to feel overwhelmed by all the uncertainties.

It took a few hours for him to finish washing all the dirty dishes and silverware in the sink, and those that Danny Connor brought in while he worked. He double checked to make sure that everything was clean and in the proper rack. With nothing more to do, he joined Danny in the kitchen.

"Hope you're not suffering dishwater hands yet," Danny joked. "This has been about as busy as we get, so looks like we're not going to overwork you on your first shift."

"I can handle it," Kohl told him. "Got anything else for me to do?"

"Not right now. We'll have a few more guys come in off the road, but they'll mostly not have anything but coffee. Just be sure we have a full rack of clean cups. May be a little early, but if you're hungry I'll fix you some breakfast."

Kohl agreed to some bacon and eggs. Danny had them on the counter in no time.

"Danny, my good man—I have to admit you put out the best breakfast fare I've had since The Pines. This is good!"

Danny Connor's big belly shook with laughter. "And I suppose you had some of the finest chefs in the country up there," he sniggered. "A man gets used to fancy cooking like that real easy."

Kohl laughed, too. He'd come to appreciate Danny's sense of humor, and the corpulent figure the fry-cook presented made him a virtual epitome of the jolly fat man. It had been hard for him to talk about prison life, but Danny's jokes had a way of loosening him up. "I doubt they have the finest of anything up there," he replied. "Except maybe the cockroaches. Only good thing I ever found was the gate out."

Danny stood across the counter, facing him. He was quiet for a moment, then said, his tone serious, "How's it going out there, Kohl? I know you've not found it easy, but sometimes you just have to give people a little time."

"Yeah, well, I'll make it. You and Mr. Spencer have been real rocks, for starters. And Cara."

"Cara's a good woman. She's had a pretty tough life, but if she's on your side she'll stick with you, whatever comes."

"I already decided that," he lied. This was something he wanted to believe, but there still were the nagging doubts he couldn't overcome.

"Well, if you're finished, maybe I ought to start introducing you to some of our regulars. Jack likes for us to make everybody feel like family. See that fellow back there in the corner? That's Bill Gentry. The old dinosaur comes in every night and has his bowl of chili and two cups of coffee."

"Seems like a serious fellow."

Danny Connor chuckled. "Very serious. He's still waiting for Bo Schembechler to run for president."

"Nobody's told him Bo's dead and gone?"

"Says he's heard rumors, but he don't believe them. Come on, I'll introduce you. He's not much of a talker, so you won't need to stop and visit."

Kohl remembered seeing the old man the first time he'd been in the Purple Onion. Playing host to customers was not something he'd expected to do, and most certainly not something he looked forward to, but if Jack Gengler wanted his employees to do it he'd see if he could manage. A non-talker would be a good place to start.

Danny Conner lead him to Bill Gentry's table, greeted the old man and introduced Kohl. "He's my new kitchen help," he explained. "Newest man on the Purple Onion staff."

Kohl extended his hand.

Bill Gentry glared at Kohl, then spoke directly to Danny Connor. "I know who he is, Danny, but I didn't know he worked here," he said. "You'll not see me darken your door again. Doc Harrell was one of my best friends."

The old man stood up and swept his arm across the table, sending everything on the surface crashing to the floor. "Oh, sorry. I'm such a clumsy old fool," he said mockingly. "I made such a mess! But I guess that's okay, Danny. Just get your new boy here down on his hands and knees and get it cleaned up. See you around."

With that, Bill Gentry stormed to the front of the room, jerked the door open almost violently, and disappeared into the darkness of the cold winter night.

THIRTEEN

IT WAS TIME for Cara, and Kohl's earlier lament over leaving her place with George Spencer when he knew she expected him to stay now seemed almost insignificant. It was Jim Endicott's off-hand comment that stuck in his craw and left him worried that he might feel better if he didn't see her this morning.

But he'd told her he would wait at the Purple Onion until she came, and he prided himself on being an honest man. He had more than enough black marks against his character; no need to earn another by compromising his integrity—especially when he already felt guilty.

There also was something deeper at play here, though, and he needed to deal with it. As he sat at a corner table with a cup of coffee to wait, he struggled to push his doubts aside. Were they actually *self-doubts*? Was he jealous of the men Jim Endicott talked about? Was he afraid he couldn't compete for Cara's attention? Was he faint-hearted now because of hurts inflicted on him in the past? There were echoes of his utter devotion to Angie in his attraction to Cara, and in the end his devotion to Angie had yielded nothing but bitter fruit.

Caught up in his own ambiguities, Kohl didn't see Cara coming until she was at his side. She hesitated briefly, then pulled out a chair on the opposite side of the table and sat down. "Well, what's your excuse?" she said. There was no bitterness in her voice. "My honey not sweet enough, or did you get a better offer?"

"I'm sorry, Cara. Mr. Spencer came by, and it seemed important to him—"

"You said that in your note. It was important to me, too, but I guess I don't count for much. Couldn't you have come back?"

"I didn't know if you wanted me to. I thought my invitation might be limited, you know, to one night."

"I don't do one-night stands, at least not *planned* one-night stands."

"I didn't mean that."

"It was kinda fun, though." Her face melted into the sweet smile he had come to adore. "You're welcome back any time you want to come, but I won't beg. We gypsies may be thieves, but we're not beggars."

"I wish you wouldn't say things like that. The gypsies being thieves part, I mean."

"Come on, Kohl. Lighten up! It was a joke. You know, beggars and thieves, out of the Bible or something. How's Jake?"

"Jake's good. He'd like to see you if you can stop by the house when you get out of here."

"We'll see. So how did your first night on the job go?"

"Some good, some bad. I'll tell you all about it if you stop by."

Cara moved her chair back from the table and stood. "Look, Kohl," she said, "I have to go to work. I can come by your house later, but I have to know: Do you really want me to? Don't pretend something you don't feel, okay?"

"Yes. I want you to come—please."

He was rewarded with another sweet smile.

<hr>

Jake went directly into his love dance the minute Kohl came through the kitchen door. He started to bark, then closed his mouth as if uncertain barking was an appropriate way to demonstrate his joy. Then he barked again, furiously, and jumped up and down and spun in circles like the proverbial dog chasing its own tail.

Kohl squatted and Jake sprang into his arms and began to lick his face.

"Missed me, didn't you?" Kohl greeted him, his own excitement equal to that demonstrated by the dog. "Sorry I'm late. I'll bet my buddy's hungry, yes? Give me another kiss and we'll see what we can do about that."

He filled Jake's bowl and got fresh water. Jake began to gobble his breakfast like a starving stray, his usual manner, and Kohl stood by like a proud father. Watching Jake eat gave him an irrational level of pleasure. He wasn't sure why. But he often thought back to the still-recent day this dog showed up at his back door and the heart-wrenching sympathy he'd felt.

He squatted again, close beside the dog. He began to stroke Jake's back. The fur was no longer matted and dirty, but soft and healthy looking. The patches of irritated skin also looked much better. Jake stopped eating just long enough to look up, his eyes aflame with love. Kohl buried his face in the fur and ruffled it with his nose.

"Who's the smartest, toughest dog there ever was?" he said loudly, as if speaking to a room filled with people. "Jake, you say? Why, of course it's Jake. Look at the way his ears stand up when I speak! Look at the curl in his tail! Jake's my buddy!"

Then, with lowered voice, speaking directly to the animal at his knees, "I'll not be late next time. I promise. But you want to know why I was late today? You do? Well, it was because I was talking to Cara. She really likes us, Jake. She wants us to come back to her house. And we will. Yes, we will. And that's a promise, too."

The change in his routine had left Kohl much more tired than he'd expected. He needed sleep. He stoked the hot coals in the fireplace and threw on a couple of the larger oak logs. Jake joined him on the mattress. The dog's eagerness to be near was flattering, but he wondered whether it also might be an indication that Jake had not slept during the night. Having to leave Jake home alone was something he was going to find most difficult, though he was confident the animal would soon adapt.

Jake squirmed closer, until his body lay against Kohl for his entire length. If there ever had been any doubt, Kohl knew now that he loved this dog as deeply as he ever had loved another living being. With this loving animal there was no deceit, only unconditional devotion.

He wanted to put all the negatives out of his thoughts entirely, or push them into the dark reaches of his subconscious, and sate himself with the closeness of Jake. He wanted peaceful sleep, resting mind as well as body. No dreams of Angie, no confused awakening to listen for the familiar sounds of prison, no misty images of a heartbroken mother waiting in vain for a son she never would see again. No guilt must intrude, no self-recrimination.

But, ah, such foolishness. In his own mind he knew that this was not to be. *You came into this life with the burden of original sin, Kohl. Three great loves. Angie would be the first. Would there ever be a perfect love? Cara? Cara? I couldn't come to her funeral. David Murray McKenzie, right with God. Her finger in their cup.* He was conflicted too many ways. Sleep would not come.

There would be no tossing and turning. Let Jake sleep in peace. He got up and went upstairs to his mother's room. The heat was stifling. He was about to open a window, then worried that a cold draft from outside might overwork the furnace he knew nothing about. This was the house in which he spent the first twenty years of his life, yet it was strange to him now. Twenty years here, twenty years in The Pines. A life wasted. And a mother's heart broken. There was too much pain in this room.

Outside, the wind was picking up and snow flurries filled the air. He wondered when Cara would come. She could stay here if the weather worsened. But could he expect her to sleep on the dirty mattress on the floor? He now had a furnace and running water. And electricity. Food in the old refrigerator and dog food in a bag for Jake. It was time to cover the old mattress with the clean linens Mr. Spencer had left.

He took a set of light blue sheets from a closet and carried them downstairs. Jake was awake, and watched closely as he put them on the mattress. The transformation this brought to the general appearance of the room surprised him. The old house could be habitable for a woman with a little more work. And money. Money he did not have.

"Life is hard, Jake," he said, not really speaking to the dog. But Jake heard his name and trotted to Kohl's side. Kohl reached down and scuffed his head and Jake went into his love dance.

"Jake, Jake, Jake!" He said this loudly, as if he wanted the world to hear. "Having Jake as my buddy makes me a lucky man!"

Looking down into Jake's adoring eyes, he added, "Yes, Jake. It really does."

FOURTEEN

CARA GIGGLED LIKE a teenager when Kohl opened the kitchen door and greeted her with open arms. She clasped him in a tight embrace and stood on tiptoes to reach his level and award him with a passionate kiss. He wanted to stand and hold her forever and let the world pass them by. He loved and wanted this woman.

She broke away to kneel and greet Jake, then stood and offered open arms again for another hug. Kohl pulled her to him and the two held each other and swayed to the rhythm of imaginary music. When she pushed him away, she kept him at arm's length and pursed her lips in a mock kiss.

"Don't pretend with me, Kohl," she said softly. "I hurt too easy."

"I've been hurt, too, Cara. I wouldn't know how to pretend, even if I wanted to. What you see is what you get."

The smile he had come to cherish lit her face. "I like what I see," she said, and giggled again. Then her expression sobered.

"I need to be up front with you," she said. "I told you I don't do one-night stands, and in general that's the truth. But there have been some. I get lonely, Kohl. Sometimes so lonely I can't stand it. There's always willing guys in the grill, and if there's somebody nice, and I've had one of those empty nights wishing so bad for another human being to be close to—well, can't you understand?"

"I understand. I get lonely, too. I guess I've been lonely most of my life."

"So you won't hold it against me? Throw it up in my face sometime when you're mad at me and call me a whore? I couldn't stand that."

Kohl pulled her to him. Their shared hunger for love, for physical connection, for complete surrender and limitless giving of themselves, for all those things lacking in their empty lives—this took control. If they were commanded by lust it was lust without blemish, lust driven by each one's desire to meld body and spirit with the other. They made love with enormous passion, and yet they loved gently and with great caring.

Unlike the night they'd made love before, this time there was no feeling of triumph. This time there had been no challenge. This time their action had been not only the manifestation of need and loneliness and simple physical longing, but also the true bonding of body, mind, and spirit.

Afterward, they lay quietly, content in their closeness. Cara was the first to speak. "Kohl, do you believe in love at first sight?"

"I do now."

"That morning you first showed up at the grill, I felt like there was something different about you. I didn't want you to go."

"I felt it, too. I wanted you close. But I was afraid it was only because, you know, I'd had no contact with women and all. You know what I mean?"

She put a finger across his lips. "Let's not even talk about anything unpleasant, okay? Let's pretend there is no past, like our lives only just began today."

Kohl cupped her hand in his and moved it against his chest. His own heart beat was palpable. He was alive and awake. This was not a dream.

"But I want to know things about you," he said. "Things about when you were a little girl and about the places you've been and all the things you've done in your whole life. I have a lot of catching up to do."

"But we can have secrets?"

Kohl laughed. This woman beside him, this woman that he had known from the beginning could be his soulmate, still was a little girl at heart. He loved her the more for it. He wanted to be a little boy again, to be her best friend and playmate, to explore all the unknowns with her and know that the trials of adulthood still were years in the future. He wanted to go back in time, and erase all that had come between then and now. And for this moment, he believed he could.

Two minutes later he was asleep.

Business was good at the Purple Onion when Kohl got there to begin his second night's work shift. The parking lot was full almost to capacity with trucks and a few cars, and most of the tables and booths were in use. Danny Connor was working at a near-frantic pace at the griddle. He barely looked up as Kohl walked past, slapped him on the shoulder, and went straight to work in the back.

There already was an intimidating backup of dirty dishes in the big sink. Kohl's first thought, though, was positive. He would be kept busy, as Danny already was, and no one would expect him to circulate in the dining room to get acquainted with regulars. He was still seething over the episode with Bill Gentry.

His initial reaction when Gentry stormed out of the grill was a general indifference. He made this clear to Danny Connor at the time: "Who the hell cares what that old fool thinks, anyway?"

Danny, although saying little, obviously had been a good deal less sanguine. Kohl hadn't been able to put the incident out of his mind, and had come to appreciate the fact that Danny had a great deal more at stake in this than he did. Not only was losing a faithful customer bad for business, but it posed the potential threat of even more serious damage. If Bill Gentry was a prominent citizen, or even if he was merely a loud-mouth who insisted his voice be heard, his complaint might reach Jack Gengler and imperil Danny's job.

He had planned to talk about all this with Cara, but once he fell asleep that opportunity had been lost. Since Gentry apparently came in only late at night and she worked days, she might not know him. But people talked. He wanted to find out all he could about this old fool who had shown him utter disrespect.

Bill Gentry would not occupy Kohl's thoughts for long on this night, though. He was thinking about Cara. He still could feel the intensity of their connection, the soft warmth of her body. He wanted to be with her again, to stay with her, to let nothing separate them, ever.

Danny Connor brought in a tray of dirty dishes and silverware and slammed it down on the long stainless steel shelf beside the deep sink. His action startled Kohl, who hadn't heard him coming.

"What the hell, Danny?" Kohl exclaimed. "Something got you riled up tonight, or just trying to bust some dishes?"

"Sorry," Danny said. "I didn't mean to bang it down so hard. But, yeah, I'm a little bit riled up. I'll tell you all about it once things slow down a little." He rushed back to the griddle, leaving Kohl with a substantially increased load of work to be done.

Wondering what Danny Connor had to tell him temporarily sidetracked Kohl's thoughts of Cara. But then his mind drifted back to the earlier hours of the day. He relived every second of their time together and it was even more beautiful than before. Her words still rang fresh in his brain. *"Do you believe in love at first sight?"* No, this was not a dream. This really happened.

But there was more. *"There's always willing guys at the grill."* Were some of those guys here right now? Was one of them Jim Endicott? Jim Endicott was hot for that gypsy waitress. Jim Endicott was one of the truckers who stopped in the Purple Onion *"just hoping to get her to stick a finger in his coffee."*

Three main loves, Mr. Spencer said. Would Cara be one of them? His perfect love? His last love? And the inescapable thought that forever lurked somewhere in his brain, *My first love was Angie.* And David Murray McKenzie bludgeoned his wife to death while she made love with another man.

But why did he have to give in to this runaway imagery that hammered without mercy inside his head? He desperately needed an interruption to break this painful train of thought and calm the turmoil in his brain, some external force to rescue him from his own damning mental process.

It came in the return of Danny Connor.

"Looks like the rush is over for now," Danny said. "Come on out and talk for a while. I'll tell you what had me so riled up. I still am, actually."

Kohl responded mechanically. Without saying anything, he put down the cup he was washing, rinsed and dried his hands, and followed Danny through the door that led into the grill's kitchen and dining room. He took a stool at the counter and waited expectantly. Danny Connor poured a cup of coffee and put it in front of him.

"Did you see Cara today?" Danny asked.

"Yes. She came by my place when she got off work."

"And?"

"And what, Danny? You got something on your mind I need to hear about?"

Danny's dead-serious demeanor gave way to a smile. "Naw," he said, "I was just hoping you had a good story for me. You know, something that would make me feel better, that's all. You and Cara are good for each other, Kohl. Make the best of that while you can. We don't always get second chances. But, hell, you know that."

"Yeah, well. Sometimes we get what looks like a good chance and it turns out to be fake, like a counterfeit bill."

"Not sure I follow you. You're not talking about Cara?"

"No, I wasn't. I might be next time, though. I was talking about this town, the second chance it's given me. I mean, some people have been great, like you, Danny. But what chance do I have as long as this place is full of Bill Gentrys and people like that? Can I even get a decent job? Damn it, Danny, I don't ask for anything special. I just want that second chance, okay?"

Danny Connor shook his head. "I don't know what to tell you," he said. "I've never walked in your shoes. Tell you what, though, next time my friend Tay is here I want you to talk to him. He's been there. One word from Tay's worth a thousand from me."

"Tay? What the hell kind of name is that?"

"How would I know? It's just what his mama named him, I guess. He's a good guy. Stops by whenever it's on his route. He knows things I don't know about getting on with your life, okay?"

"I'll talk to him. Thank you, Danny. You're a friend. So now you can tell me, what's got you all riled up tonight? Anything I can help you with?"

"I hope it doesn't have anything to do with you. Jack was in earlier tonight and told me some things I hated to hear. Seems like Rasmusan—Sam Rasmusan, the guy who owns this place—wants some changes I'd hate to see. I'm gonna try to stop worrying about it. A lot of these big ideas never get any further than talk."

"You can always hope," Kohl told him. "But it wouldn't be bad if he started by paving that damned parking lot, would it? There's potholes out there deep enough to swallow a horse."

"I won't argue that. Wasn't any mention of the parking lot in what I heard, though." His voice dropped almost to a whisper. "Damn, don't look up. We've got company. What the hell is he doing out here this time of night?"

Ignoring the advice, Kohl turned and looked back. Deputy Scott Sobeski was coming through the front door.

FIFTEEN

SCOTT SOBESKI APPROACHED the counter where Danny Connor stood facing him and Kohl sat, his back turned to the approaching deputy. He walked fast, as if on an urgent mission. He put his cap and gloves on the counter and climbed onto a stool beside Kohl. He clapped his bare hands together, then put them up to his mouth and blew on them.

"You got anything hot back there?" he asked.

"You want coffee, or what?" Danny Connor responded. "Coffee's always hot."

"Yeah, get me some. Maybe a couple of cups of hot coffee on my insides will warm me up. It's colder than a witch's tit out there tonight." He turned to Kohl, so close their elbows rubbed. "Somebody told me you worked here. I thought old Jack had higher standards than that."

Before Kohl could speak, Danny answered him, "Jack knows what he's doing. This man is a good worker. You come in here for coffee or to harass my staff, Sobeski?" He shoved a cup in front of the deputy and poured hot coffee from a carafe. "Coffee's on the house for officers of the law. Can I get you anything else?"

"This will do."

Sobeski picked up the coffee and started to drink, then quickly put it down and slapped the counter with an open hand. "Damn, that's hot!" he exclaimed. "You trying to blister my tongue, Danny boy?"

"Purple Onion coffee is always hot. You wouldn't want it any other way."

"You know you can get sued if it's too hot and somebody gets burned."

Danny Connor's face reddened. "We ain't burned anybody yet," he said. "But maybe those truck drivers are just a tough lot. How come you're out here this time of night, anyway?"

"I volunteer for the night shift every chance I get. More action at night."

"Oh, yeah? What kind of action you seen tonight? Criminals running free in our streets these days?"

Kohl slid from his seat and started around the end of the counter. "I need to get back to work, Danny," he said.

"Just a minute!" Sobeski demanded. "I want a word with you, Kohl. I saw Cara's Jeep at your place. Didn't I warn you to stay away from that gypsy?"

Kohl stopped short and turned to face the deputy. Danny Connor stepped to his side, as if making ready to get between the two men. "Sobeski, you're wasting your time spying on me," Kohl said. "I am not doing anything illegal, and who comes to my house is none of your business."

"It is if you are associating with criminals. I guarantee you that gypsy has a record some place. It probably won't take much digging to find it, and when I do I'll be coming after you both. I'm not giving you another warning." He stood and put on his cap and picked up his gloves from the counter. "Thanks for the coffee, Danny boy. I'll be stopping in again soon."

Deputy Sobeski left the grill, met by a blast of icy wind and a swirling surge of blowing snow as he went out the door.

"He's an idiot," Danny Connor said.

"Yeah, but an idiot wearing a badge," Kohl replied. "That's a dangerous combination."

———————————

Kohl's anticipation built as he waited for Cara. Even having to deal with Deputy Scott Sobeski had barely diminished the bliss of this day. He truly had felt as if he and Cara were one—a notion he'd always considered a somewhat silly cliché before. He couldn't wait to see her again.

She was early. He rushed to meet her the instant he saw her coming.

"Hey, good-looking man," she greeted him. And she offered that pretty smile.

"I've been waiting for you," he said, and opened his arms to invite an embrace. She leaned against him and they stood holding each other tightly. "This is the way I'd like to start my days forever."

Cara led the way to a booth near the front of the grill.

"Sit and wait while I get us some coffee," she told him. "I'll be back in a second."

Kohl slid into the booth, taking the bench that faced toward the back so that he could see her going to the counter and watch her as she came back. She quickly organized a tray and headed back. When she got there she tended the table like a waitress, pouring cups of steaming coffee for each of them before sitting opposite him.

"Jesus, it's cold out there this morning," she said. "I thought I might freeze to death before I got in from the parking lot. Are you sure you can make it home on a bicycle?"

"Just thinking about yesterday will keep me warm, Cara."

She reached across the table and took his hand. "I'll never forget yesterday," she said. "We were meant to be together. I'm selfish, Kohl. I don't want to give you up. Ever."

"I feel the same way. Yesterday was—"

He was interrupted by the other waitress on the job with Cara, who rushed up beside their table and said, somewhat sharply, "We gotta get to work now, hon. There's people coming in."

"Kohl, meet Cindy," Cara said. And to Cindy, "Look, I'll be there in a minute. There's only one table occupied. Take care of them, and I'll catch the next one who comes in. Okay?"

Cindy's irritation was apparent, but she turned and headed toward the waiting customers without saying anything more.

"I'm sorry," Cara said. "She don't mean to be rude. She's just always afraid we'll get in trouble with Jack and get fired. But I guess I do need to go to work."

"When you get a chance, ask Danny about Sobeski. He dropped by to enjoy coffee with us, and just happened to mention your name."

"That sleazy little weasel!"

"On second thought, don't ask Danny. I'll tell you about it later. I wish you could come home with me. Will you come by again when you get off?"

She squeezed his hand as she slipped out from behind the table and stood, then leaned in and whispered, "Just don't lock the door, okay?"

Even though their separation would be temporary, Kohl already missed her. He was tempted to keep his seat and stay in the grill for another hour or two just to keep her near. But common sense prevailed. He needed to get home to take care of Jake and try to catch at least a bit of sleep before Cara came in the afternoon. And he missed Jake, too.

He quickly finished the coffee Cara had poured, put things back on the tray she'd brought them on, and carried them toward the back. He caught her eye and waved. She waved back and blew him a kiss.

Jake was waiting just inside the door, whining his urgency for relief. He squeezed through when Kohl had it half open. Kohl waited, and the dog soon was finished outside and back in, promptly going into its love dance and offering soft barks of welcome. Kohl picked up the dog and squeezed it to his chest. Jake took advantage of his new position to launch an episode of face-licking.

"Who is this?" Kohl demanded. "Why, it's Jake!"

He put the dog down and got fresh food and water, which Jake accepted after a moment of hesitation. It looked as if he were uncertain whether eating and drinking should claim higher rank than continuing the intimacy with Kohl. Once the decision was made, though, he attacked his food like a hungry wolf.

Kohl was desperate to get to a hot shower. The ride home from the Purple Onion on Danny Connor's old bicycle had been hazardous to the point of danger. Old Church Road was ice-coated, and strong wind gusts threatened to blow him over. Given the frigid temperature, he worried that a simple crash could lead to an injury severe enough he might freeze to death before help happened by.

Cold always made his bum knee hurt more. Climbing the stairs would be a challenge, but once he was in the shower the hot water would bring some relief. Jake was still eating so he didn't wait, but went straight to the stairs and made his way up to the second floor. The bad knee was throbbing with pain by the time he reached the landing.

The hot shower had the effect he hoped for. He cut it short, eager to get a few hours of sleep before Cara came in the afternoon. When he got downstairs, Jake was asleep on the mattress in the middle of the living room floor.

"Okay, little guy, I know what's going on," he said, lying down close to the animal. "You're not sleeping while I'm gone, right? What are we going to do about that?" But even if he had expected an answer, it would have come too late. Kohl was asleep, himself, almost as soon as his head hit the pillow.

There were no bad dreams this morning. Even as the wind outside howled menacingly, Kohl dreamed of warm summer days with his mother and sisters. Sweet images of family gatherings in the old house faded in and out, trading places with scenes in the cherry orchards with Mr. Spencer. And then Cara was there, too, out of place in his real world but normal in the wonderland of dreams. He was magically transformed into an adult and he and Cara were alone and found beautiful places to make love. There was no Angie here, no Pines penitentiary, no Deputy Scott Sobeski. His world was tranquil and in it he was at peace.

He was still sleeping when Cara tapped softly on the back door. Jake heard her and woke him, then ran to greet her with happy barks of welcome. Kohl's knee had stiffened while he slept and he walked with a pronounced limp which she noticed immediately after their long embrace and an interval of passionate kisses.

"That's something new," she said. It was a statement of simple fact, but her tone spoke of concern.

"Nope," Kohl said. "It's something I've lived with for many years. Just a little worse right now."

"Is it bad? A serious injury, I mean."

"Nothing worth writing home about. I got my knee busted up a little in a prison riot, but it doesn't hurt me much most of the time."

"You were in a prison riot? I can't believe you'd get involved in something like that. I thought it was the gang bangers that started riots."

Kohl took her by the hand and laughed. He shook his head in what he intended as a sign of commiseration. "I'll bet you don't even know what a gang banger is," he told her. "And for my part, I couldn't help getting involved. It started in the yard while I was on exercise time. A guard evidently thought I was an instigator, or more likely just didn't give a damn one way or the other. Anyway, he took advantage of the situation to give me a whack across the knee with a billy club."

"Did they do anything for you? Anything to fix it?"

"Not really. A couple of x-rays, and said there was nothing to do about it. A little bone chip or two floating around in there or something like that. I just consider it a souvenir of my years at The Pines."

"If it hurts very much I have pain medicine left from when I broke a toe last summer. I can get it for you."

"No, I'm okay. You broke a toe? How in—"

"I'm clumsy. I tripped myself up getting out of the Jeep. You don't get a lot of sympathy for a broke toe, but it hurt like hell."

Cara slipped an arm around his waist and pulled herself tightly against his side. "Make love to me, Kohl," she said. "I don't want to think about you in a place like that or me with a broke toe and all. Nothing from the past, just us, here and now."

He accepted her invitation. They shared the mattress on the floor with Jake, who showed a profound interest in what was going on but made no effort to interfere.

SIXTEEN

KOHL PANTED LIKE an exhausted runner at the end of a long-distance race. Cara giggled, turned on her side to face him, and pulled herself close. Her bare breasts pushed against his chest. Jake apparently had given up on chances of any activity he could be a part of and was asleep on the floor beside the mattress, snoring loudly.

"You're all wore out," Cara teased. "I think maybe I'm working you too hard. I don't want to use you up too fast!"

Kohl tried to growl like an animal but failed miserably. The sound he made was more like a grunt. "I've only begun, Miss Cara," he said, flipping himself over on his side and taking a breast in his mouth.

She slapped at him in mock rejection. "Kohl, you're just like eve ry other man. You're all still little boys who never wanted to give up your mama's tits."

He pulled back, raised up on an elbow, and leaned in to kiss her on the forehead. "And how would you know about every other man?"

Cara sobered. "I was joking. Don't you know that, Kohl? Please don't think I consider myself an expert on men. Okay?"

There was a note of pleading in her voice. He wanted to say he didn't care, her past didn't matter. But he did care. Jim Endicott's words about "that gypsy waitress" had stuck with him. How many truckers made it a point to stop by the Purple Onion just to see her?

"Maybe you are," he said. "You admitted to one-night stands, and you want to keep secrets. How many one-night stands are we talking about?"

Cara pulled back. "You said you wouldn't bring it up like that," she reminded him. There were tears in her eyes. "I can't stand it if you think of me that way. I'm not a whore. You said you get lonely, too. But when I lie down with you it's not because I'm lonely. I love you, Kohl. If you don't believe that, or if you don't understand the difference, we can't make this work. Do you want me to go?"

Kohl hated himself for the things he'd said. If only he could take back his words, erase them and make them go away. Cara was standing now, pulling on her clothes almost frantically. The hurt was visible on her face. He stood, too, and held his arms open hoping she would step into them and let him clasp her to him and hold her forever. She made no move toward him. He felt helpless and confused.

"I didn't mean that," he said. "I love you, too. Please don't go, Cara. I want you to stay. Please."

"If you don't trust me, sooner or later you'll throw me out. I couldn't stand the hurt of that. I'd rather not have been connected at all than have you drop me like an old wore out pair of shoes. Please don't do that to me, Kohl. Do you really mean what you say, or will you wake up tomorrow and think what a fool you was?"

"I was a fool just now. You were right. The future's all that matters now."

She smiled her beautiful smile. "I've lived most of my life on hope," she said. "Most of the time that's all I had. If I can't take a chance on hope, I just as well jump off a bridge somewhere. I hope you love me the way I love you, Kohl. That means the past don't matter. I want to be with you. I'll take you the way you are if you'll take me the way I am. Is that a deal?"

"Yes."

There was no need for elaboration. She came into his arms and they stood together tightly in a long embrace. It was Kohl who finally had to separate. He did so reluctantly, but the pain in his knee forced him to change his position. Cara apparently sensed his problem.

"Oh, I'm sorry," she said. "I oughtn't to keep you standing."

"I'm okay. But it'd be fine with me to lay back down."

"Are you ready again? You're a hungry man, Kohl!"

He couldn't tell if she was serious. And he was hungry for her again, but he was not ready. "I always want you, but I don't think I've recovered from the sensational game we just played," he told her. "Maybe give me another minute—"

"You ain't going to be ready in another minute, either," she teased. "Nobody wants you to play hurt. It may be kind of dull, but looks like we have to settle for talk. You up for that?"

"I am if we can talk about you. There are lots of things I want to know. You don't have to tell me your secrets, but I want to know everything about you that you're willing to tell."

"But I'm not very interesting."

"Tell me about your brother."

"He's dead. He was killed on his motorcycle someplace in Tennessee eight years ago. I didn't even know about it for three or four months. Nobody knew where to find me."

Kohl squeezed her hand and kissed her on the nose. "I'm sorry," he said. "Was he the only family you had left?"

"Maybe still some cousins in Georgia, but I don't know for sure. Only thing I know for sure is that I've been alone for a long time."

"Cara, can we travel? You talk about Tennessee and Georgia and places like that where I've never been. I've not even been to places like Mackinac Island. I always thought when I got free I would go to places like that. You know, places I always heard about when I was a kid."

Cara touched a finger to her lips, then pressed it on his in a mock kiss. "I wish I'd been a little girl with you," she said. "And I wouldn't have been any place, either. But yeah, we can travel. I've moved around all my life. I think I have been here longer than any place else I've ever lived."

"Where would you like to go?"

"We can go to Mackinac Island, and maybe even stay at the Grand Hotel. If you want to, I mean. And I want to go to the Upper Peninsula. When I first come here I kept hearing about the 'you pee' and I didn't know what it was. Even after I found out it was a place. Maybe just a big woods where—"

"But I want to see the rest of the country, like you have. I'd like to see mountains, like Tennessee. And I want to see Alabama, wherever it was you were a little girl. How would we live, though? I mean, we'd have to have money, and if we didn't stay in one place how could we get jobs?"

"I know what we could do. We could get a truck—one of them big ones you can live in. They've got beds, so one of us would sleep while the other one drove and that way we'd just keep moving and make good money. We could travel all over the country. Some of the trucks I've seen have like whole rooms in them, even with refrigerators and televisions."

Kohl suddenly stiffened. "I don't want to hear about all the trucks you've been in."

Cara pulled away. "Damn it, Kohl, don't start that again! I know what you're thinking, and it's a bunch of shit. I worked in a truck washing and cleaning place in Ohio. I had to get inside and clean them, like a maid or something. Okay?"

"I'm sorry. I didn't mean that."

But he had broken the happy mood. They were talking about the future, making plans. These were the things they would do. Together. No more loneliness, no more living in the past. Why couldn't he go with that, relish a life with Cara, look ahead to all the things he'd dreamed of doing as a free man?

Deep down, he knew the answer. He had made plans with Angie, too.

Jake was awake now, and wanted attention. Cara moved away so the animal could squeeze in between them. The dog's presence quickly lightened the mood again. Kohl scuffed him on the head and Cara tickled his belly.

"Wherever we go," Cara said, "Jake has to go with us. I know you love him, and I do, too."

Kohl held the dog's muzzle in the palm of his hand, grasping gently with fingers and thumb, and leaned in so that their noses almost touched. Jake's eyes fixed on his.

"Look at the way his ears turn up when I speak," Kohl said. "Jake's the smartest dog in Michigan. Everybody knows that. And Jake's my buddy! And that makes old Kohl the luckiest man in the world."

"You two!" Cara exclaimed.

"I'll bet he's hungry, and I'm nearly out of dog food. Seems like that bag went down real fast."

Cara offered a solution. While she was there with transportation, they could go to Baum Farm Supply and load up on food for Jake. It was too cold for Kohl to go on his bicycle, and if he was riding the bike he couldn't carry much. She'd feel better if Jake had the added security of an extra bag or two. Didn't he agree?

Kohl did agree, and quickly said so.

Jake reacted to the mention of his name. He cocked his head and looked first at Cara and then at Kohl with the quizzical expression they had come to recognize; he would ask questions if he could. Cara assured him that he would not be disappointed with the outcome of their discussion. And he would get a ride in the Jeep.

A few minutes later they were on the way.

As she drove, Cara reminded Kohl that he was supposed to tell her something about Sobeski. "Only if it's important, though," she added. "I don't really care what that little shit says."

"He made it sound important. He thinks you're on a police wanted list somewhere, and says he's determined to find it. Then he can hustle me for associating with known criminals. That man must lay awake nights trying to think of ways to get me back behind bars."

"I won't deny I've done things I ain't proud of, you know, just to survive. And I've spent time in lots of different places. I can't be sure there's not an old wants or warrants list out there someplace with my name on it, Kohl. So if that cocky little rooster don't have nothing better to do than try to dig up something on me, he might do it. But I don't lose no sleep over it."

"Let's don't worry about it," Kohl said. "Nobody's going to take time to mess with his petty little bullying. Maybe his new game will keep him at his desk and we won't have to see him every time we turn around. Hey, this might turn out to be a good thing!"

"Only good thing that man's ever gonna do for us is disappear off the face of the earth! But we're here. Enough of Sobeski, okay?"

The Baum parking lot was sparsely occupied, but there were more people inside than they might have expected. They went straight to the pet supplies aisle and got two different kinds of dog food. Kohl hadn't thought of anything else they needed. Turning the shopping cart toward the check-out counter, he almost bumped into an old couple coming behind them.

"Sorry," he said. "Looks like I'm a careless driver today. Excuse me."

"I know who you are," the old man said. "I hope they don't ever let you drive in this town again. I don't know why they ever let you out!"

Cara put a gentle hand on Kohl's arm, but turned to the other man with a scathing glare. "You're a stupid old fool," she said angrily. "Nobody cares what you think!"

Kohl was still seething when they got back to the old house. Even Jake's excitement over his new food bags did little to assuage his anger. Cara had said little on the way home, but now she opened up with a stream of profanities that surprised Kohl by their virulence.

"I can't stand these stupid people!" she declared. "That old man's not fit to scrape your boots. How do you take it all the time?"

Her outburst had a remarkable effect on Kohl. Cara's opinion was far more important to him than that of some stranger in the farm supply store. She was on his side, and right now hardly anything else mattered.

"By doing things that make me forget about old fools like him," he told her. "Things like making love to gypsy women."

"Oh, yeah? You know any gypsy women who might be interested?"

"I'm about to find out."

"You don't have to look no further, good-looking man!"

They had discovered that each had an almost insatiable appetite for the other. This might not last forever, but they would make the best of it now and relish it as far as it stretched into their future.

Cara stayed until it was time for Kohl to go to work at the Purple Onion. She insisted on driving him in the Jeep, fearing the bitter cold was dangerous. He gave in reluctantly. Jake sat in the middle of the kitchen floor as they readied to leave.

"Stay here in the warm and get some sleep tonight," Kohl told the dog. "I won't be late in the morning. Miss Cara here will be bringing me home. Doesn't that have a kinda nice sound?"

SEVENTEEN

FACING A MOUND of dirty dishes and silverware, Kohl worked hard and fast. His frustration over things he could not control was mounting again. He had come to doubt that he ever would be a truly free man. His past would be part of his life story forever, and it seemed as if his past still intruded every day.

He had given up all hope of universal acceptance in this place he called home. Those who hated him for what he'd done never would stop hating. It was time to take a hard look at his chances for a normal life.

There was no way to avoid the haters, of course. He never could be sure in advance who they were. But to the greatest extent possible, he needed to center his world in a circle of friends like Danny Connor and Mr. Spencer, who accepted him knowing who he was and what he had done. And Cara. Cara surely was to be the brightest star in his cloudy sky.

But first, he had to get past the doubts and have faith in this woman who had come to mean everything to him. He was ashamed of his behavior earlier in the day. He had hurt Cara, and this was the last thing he wanted to do. Why could he not accept what lay before him at face value, ignoring the rumors and fantasies planted in his head by others who could not possibly know the true heart of this woman the way he did?

Self-doubts, self-recriminations. Kohl sensed a very real danger these were becoming a mainstay of his mundane patterns of thinking. The darker shadows of his past would not fade away.

Danny Connor leaned through the cold-room door and called him. "Hey, Kohl, you about caught up back here?"

Kohl welcomed the intrusion. "Yeah, Danny," he answered. "You're not too hard to keep up with tonight, after I got caught up. What's happening out front?"

"My buddy Tay's here. I thought you could talk to him about second chances, remember? Take a break and I'll get the two of you together."

Kohl dried his hands and followed Danny, glad to exit the cramped confines of the cold-room. Danny led him to a booth at the front of the grill. The man seated there greeted them with a wide smile. Kohl remembered seeing him in the Purple Onion before.

"Tay, meet Kohl," Danny said. "I'll leave you two alone to talk about your common interests. Let me know if you need anything."

The man extended a hand. "Hello, Kohl," he said pleasantly. "Have a seat."

Kohl slid onto the bench opposite the truck driver, returning the greeting "There's supposed to be something special about you," he added. "Danny didn't tell me what it was."

"Hey, man, nothing special, okay? My route brings me through here all the time and Danny considers me a regular. Says it's like old home week when he sees me coming. He tells me you and me have something in common, meaning we both spent a little time as guest of the state. This is about second chances, right?"

Kohl was surprised and a bit angry that Danny would spread the word about him this openly. "Yeah, well. Should I dance on the table, or what?" he said sarcastically. "Being back on the street doesn't ex-actly make us heroes to our fellow citizens. Or maybe your home-coming brought out a big celebration I didn't get."

Tay laughed, a big laugh that carried across the near-empty room. "Can't say they called out the high school band and threw me a parade," he said. "But there were a few old friends who hadn't turned their backs on me. Anyway, I expect you were as happy to get back on the street as I was. That's time I'd be glad to erase from my life if I could."

"Well, we got that in common. Where'd you spend time at?"

"Menard," Tay said. "Officially, the Menard Correctional Center at Chester, Illinois, on the high east bank of the mighty Mississippi

River. A luxury resort that shows up in your nightmares for the rest of your life. What was your address?"

"The Pines. One of Michigan's finest, a ways up the road."

"Max security, right?"

"Oh, yeah. Highest ratio of guards to prisoners our honorable corrections department could manage. So that's what he expected us to talk about?"

"Straight up, Danny said getting back in the stream had been tough on you. He knows you're discouraged. He just thought it might be good if I talked to you about it. You know, somebody who's been there, show you it can be done."

Kohl was happy to sit. He felt like he'd been standing on the hard cold-room floor for ten or twelve hours. "Danny's a good guy," he said. "So go ahead. Lay your big success story on me. You put in your time and now they want you to run for governor."

Tay's smile evaporated. He looked Kohl squarely in the eyes. "Save your shit for somebody else," he said firmly. "I'll help you if I can, because Danny asked me to. But I'd just as soon sit here with a finger up my nose and lick my spoon as to waste time on you if you're gonna give me attitude. Or maybe your lily white ass is too precious to think you might learn something from a black man. It wouldn't be the first time I've got that and it won't be the last. So let me know if you want to play nice, or get the hell out of my sight. Are we straight on that, Mister Kohl?"

Kohl immediately regretted his rude behavior, and was ashamed that he could have given Tay reason to suspect he might be racist. In his entire life, he had never heard anyone in his family make a racist comment and one of the few clear memories of his father centered on a day there was modest outrage in the community over a well-publicized racist incident. His father was angry and lectured Kohl and his sisters on the evils of racism or, for that matter, any kind of discrimination. It was almost as if he still could hear his father's words.

"By the grace of God, we are all the same color inside," his father proclaimed sternly. "A heart inside black skin or red skin or yellow skin or skin striped like a rainbow beats the same as yours and mine. There is only one true race and that is the *human* race. Do not ever forget what I say!"

How much effect his father's words had had on his own point of view was something Kohl hadn't thought about, but he hated discrimination and he'd been unprepared for and saddened by overt examples he had witnessed in prison. He was determined to persuade Tay that he was not racist.

What could he say? "I'm sorry," was his starting point, and his apology was genuine.

"So do we have anything to talk about, or not? Danny said he most likely would need you back in the kitchen in half an hour or so."

"I really am sorry, Tay. I apologize. I was rude, and that's not my style. I'd like to hear what you have to say. I mean that."

Tay's wide smile returned. "There's no magic words, man," he said. "It was rough on me, too. But I got through it okay and now I got my own life back. I don't pretend to be an example of any kind. You don't walk down the mean streets of Gary, Indiana—that's my home town, man—you don't walk around Gary and hear anybody say, 'Tay's a big man, now' or 'Tay's got it all together.' But there's at least a few people who know me and respect me for what I've done."

"Danny Connor says you're a good guy."

Tay laughed again. "Danny don't know me that well," he said. "But here's my point: I own my own truck now, I make a decent living, I'm not watching in the rear-view mirror all the time to see who's coming behind me. That didn't come easy. But I stuck with it. Nobody owes you respect, Kohl. You have to earn it."

The big truck driver's words had a ring of authenticity. Tay had traveled the same path he had and spoke from experience. No matter how sympathetic people like Danny Connor and Mr. Spencer were, they would never see the world through his eyes. There was no question that this man knew where he was coming from.

"A chance to earn it is all I've ever wanted," he said. "Do you think guys like Danny, who've never been inside, do you think there's any way they can possibly know what it's like? You're out of the real world for so long you forget what the real world is. You're like a chicken in a cage and you don't even know where the other chickens go and what they do all day."

"Oh, yeah. Tell me about it, man," Tay said. "And I'll go you one better. You're a rooster in a cage and all the hens are running loose among other roosters. You know what I'm saying?"

"Sure I do. But I don't want to go there."

"Hard making it back into the hens' nests, right?"

Kohl felt his chest begin to tighten. He'd been serious that this was an area of discussion he didn't want to get into. Any talk of his relationship with women inevitably led back to his recognition that no matter what happened from this day forward, the course of his life had been unalterably set by his link with Angie. But this was not something he cared to share with Tay.

"Yeah, well, I just let nature take its course," he said, hoping to move talk completely away from the topic. "But, hey, I got a question for you. I'm fascinated by your name. Where did 'Tay' come from, if you don't mind me getting a bit personal?"

Tay's face lit up again with his big smile. "I don't mind," he answered. "Lots of people ask about it. See, my mama wanted to name me Jean, after the guy in that French book she liked so much. You know, Jean Valjean, or whatever. Ever heard of it?"

"Yeah, I remember it from high school. And that guy went to prison for something, didn't he?"

"Hey, I never read the damned book. I don't know anything about it. But, anyway, my dad wanted to name me after my grandpa, whose name was Taylor. So they got real clever and compromised, so to speak, and named me Tay-Jean. Ain't that a hell of a name!"

Now the big smile was on Kohl's face. "I like it!" he declared. "Makes you sound like a movie star or something."

"Except that nobody in this country says 'Jean' that way. They say 'Gene.' You follow me?"

"Yeah, but I don't see why it's a problem."

"When they see it in writing, they think it's a girl's name. Every time I had a new teacher they'd be looking around the room for a girl. When I was about ten years old I decided to ditch the last half and just be Tay. Been that ever since."

Kohl's outlook had brightened. He liked this man. He was envious of Tay's optimistic view of life. Might he realistically hope to gain a more hopeful view, himself, through this connection? It wouldn't come from this brief contact, but maybe if they spent more time together there was at least some modest promise.

Tay might have been reading his mind. "Look, Kohl," he said, "you have to go back to work now and I have to get back on the road. I like you, man. I want you to see a little more of the sunshine and a lot less of the dark. You know what I mean? Maybe you can find time to do a little road time with me one of these days."

Danny Connor was busy at the griddle when Kohl got to the back of the grill, but looked up and asked, "You like old Tay?"

"Yes. I do."

"Feel better about second chances?"

"Yeah, I guess. Tay's been on the inside, so he knows what he's talking about. But his story might be different if he had to try to get a second chance in this town."

EIGHTEEN

CARA'S PLACE WAS warm and cozy. When she insisted that he and Jake come home with her, Kohl felt obligated to accept. She had spent the last several afternoons with them in the old house and said she was commencing to feel at home there. But she liked the thought of having Kohl sleeping with her in her own bed. She and Jake were becoming fast friends, too, and she wanted the dog to know that he always would be safe and sound in her place as well as at home.

"If something happened and you didn't make it home some morning, he'd be lost," she told Kohl. "I love that the two of you are so close, but sometimes I worry that he's too attached to you. Do you ever think about that?"

"Yes, it has crossed my mind. I tell him I'll always be there for him, and that's what I intend to do. But you're right. If something happened to me, I don't know what he'd do."

"But you know I'd take him," she said.

"I would want you to. I know he loves you, too. Another thing me and him have in common."

He was rewarded by her prettiest smile and a quick little kiss on the cheek. "Sweet talk will get you anything you want, handsome man," she teased. And then, more seriously, "You'd miss him as much as he'd miss you."

"Absolutely! I can't begin to tell you how much the little guy means to me. Sometimes I feel like there was a reason he showed up at my door when he did. I mean, I was about as low and lonely as a man can get, and here came this poor homeless creature, cold and hungry, just looking for shelter. He asks for so little."

"My daddy used to say God give us animals to keep us humble. Kohl, do you believe in God?"

She waited pensively for an answer.

This was Cara being Cara. He was fascinated by the way she often took his words and led him in a different direction. In another person, he might have seen this as fuzzy thinking, but in Cara he saw it simply as her lively curiosity ready to pop out at the slightest provocation. Even if he had no other interest in this woman, talking with her always would be fun.

"I'm not sure," he told her, wanting very much to offer a thoughtful response. "Mostly, I'm confused. I guess there has to be a God, but I don't know how He works. The chaplain said God doesn't take sides, like He's neither for us nor against us. Mr. Spencer says God loves us and is merciful and wants to save us from our sinful ways. It seems to me that those don't match up."

"Everybody's got their own opinion. Don't you think maybe we all get to decide for ourselves?"

"I don't know."

And now he was sorry again, and felt somewhat foolish. It was as if she had been excited over real discussion of a subject important to her and he had not held up his end of the conversation. He wanted to do better. Cara had started to speak, but he interrupted.

"Yeah, I think they do. The chaplain said God's too busy to come looking for us, so we have to make the first contact. So wouldn't this kind of leave it up to us to figure out where He was and how to speak to Him? Like, if you feel like it you can throw yourself face-down in the dirt and ask God to pardon the interruption, but please have mercy on you. Or you can stand up straight and look up to the heavens and yell, 'Yo, God. How 'bout giving me a hand down here?' And I suppose some guys would—"

Cara elbowed him in the ribs. "Stop it!" she demanded. "Kohl, you break me up sometimes. But you better be careful. You don't mess with God like that. You and me have got enough trouble. We don't need to get God mad at us!"

He pulled her close against him. "I just hope God's not watching us too close right now," he said. "He might be embarrassed seeing us do what I have in mind, gypsy woman."

"Then put your dog in the back room and get yourself ready for some real action, cowboy! This gypsy woman's gonna be waiting."

At long last, Kohl had stopped worrying about his competence as a lover. He might not be a Casanova, but it was apparent that he and Cara were well paired and that was all that mattered. The first time they had sex, when she was the aggressor and he never had experienced the act before, he had been sure his performance was inadequate. Learning that she had been with other men caused him even greater doubt. But now, their bond was love and he was no longer concerned about his ability. He found sex without the self-doubt to be exquisitely satisfying. He believed that Cara felt the same. And to his great relief, sex with Angie seldom showed up in his dreams anymore.

His outlook was bright when it came time for Cara to take him to work. He went through his usual routine with Jake, scuffing his head and ears, stroking his back, taking his muzzle in hand and rubbing noses. Jake's eyes were aflame with devotion. He performed his love dance several times over.

Kohl poured more food into the dog's bowl and checked his water. There were crumbs in the bottom of the water bowl, and he took it to the sink and dumped it, refilled it with fresh water, and returned it to its familiar place on the kitchen floor. Jake followed him around and sampled both the food and the water as soon as they were in place.

"I think he wants to show his appreciation," Cara said. "And he wants to be sure you see it."

Jake sat proudly as Kohl began his pretentious performance: "Jake's the smartest, toughest dog there ever was. Look at the way his ears stand up when I speak! And Jake's my buddy! And that makes old Kohl the luckiest man in the world!"

The dog knew the routine. As Kohl finished, he lay down near the door and waited. He was ready to go when Cara opened the door, and eagerly ran ahead as she and Kohl went to the Jeep.

Strong gusts of wind battered the canvas cab of the Jeep as they drove. There were places where the road was icy and treacherous.

"I worry about you driving back by yourself, Cara," Kohl said. "If you got stuck out here who knows how long it might be before anybody came along to help."

"But I always carry my cell phone. And don't forget, my guardian is riding in the back seat."

"Your backseat guardian probably would sleep through it all. And by the way, I want you to show me your cell phone one of these days and teach me how to use it."

They were on Old Church Road now, and almost in front of Kohl's house. The windshield of the drafty old Jeep was partially masked by condensation, with not enough engine heat yet to make the defrosters effective. Cara leaned forward to clear the glass with a gloved hand.

"Oh, my good lord!" she exclaimed. "Can you believe this?"

A police vehicle sat across the driveway to the old house, facing oncoming traffic. Just as Cara saw it, its lights started flashing. "What am I supposed to do?" she said. "Am I supposed to stop, or what?"

Her question was answered when Deputy Scott Sobeski stepped out from behind the police car and held up a hand signaling stop. When she did, he was at her door almost immediately. She lowered a window and he aimed a bright light in her face.

"You're blinding me!" Cara complained. "What the hell do you want, Sobeski?"

"The sheriff's worried that there's more traffic out here, and wonders if all the new drivers are properly licensed and all that. Sent me out here on patrol to find out. Since I know you, I'm going to trust that your driver's license is in order and not even ask to see it, okay?" He shined the light on Kohl. "Maybe you don't know it, but you are in the company of a man just released from prison for a heinous crime. I'd have to consider him still dangerous. Maybe you need to be more careful who you keep company with."

While Kohl was fumbling mentally for a response, the deputy pointed his bright light into the back of the Jeep, directly in Jake's eyes. The dog jumped around the seat and barked excitedly.

"I hope you keep this vicious dog penned up, Kohl," Sobeski said. "He's going to attack somebody one of these days, and if that happens the county will take him. Do you understand what I'm saying?"

The threat to Jake was more than Kohl could take and stay silent.

"Oh, I understand, Sobeski, but—"

Cara put a hand on his knee as she interrupted. "Jake is no more vicious than your grandma's teapot," she told Sobeski. "You know you don't have no reason to think he'd hurt somebody. You just want to harass Kohl. Now can we go on?"

There was clear anger in the deputy's voice. "I'd be careful what I said if I were you. This Jeep looks like it's seen better days. I'd sure hate to have you end up in court, but if I just happened to inspect your vehicle and I just happened to find a faulty taillight or something, I would have no choice but to write you a ticket. You think I ought to take a look?"

"There's nothing wrong with my Jeep! All we want is to go on our way," Cara told him. "We didn't cause you any trouble and we don't want no trouble, okay?"

Deputy Sobeski took a step back, away from the window. "You can go," he said, "but you might want to give more thought to who you drive around town with. Associating with a known criminal . . ."

His final words were wasted as Cara jerked the Jeep's transmission into gear and gunned the engine. Neither of them spoke until the vehicle was up to speed, by which time they were halfway to the Purple Onion. Kohl was shaking with anger.

"I swear, I wish that little bully would get run over by a truck or something," he declared.

Cara burst out laughing. "I'm sorry," she said, "but it hit me how that sounded, coming from a dangerous criminal. I'd think you'd want to shoot him or bash his head with a sledgehammer or something, you know, given how vicious you are. Maybe I don't need to be scared, after all."

Despite his anger, her good humor brought Kohl around. He laughed, too. He put a hand on hers. "Miss Cara," he said dramatically, "what you have to fear from me has nothing to do with guns or sledgehammers. But I give you fair warning. I *will* be coming after you!"

Cara drove through the Purple Onion parking lot and stopped at the door. "Goodbye kiss!" she demanded, putting a finger to her lips. Kohl obliged. He looked back at Jake, and saw that the dog was fast asleep.

"I'm a little bit worried that you'll run into Sobeski again," he said to Cara. "What would you do?"

"Don't worry about me. I can handle that little chicken. Get in there and get to work. I'll see you in the morning."

Kohl climbed out of the Jeep and she drove off.

Inside, he found the grill almost deserted. Danny Connor and Jack Gengler sat at a table near the back drinking coffee. Danny saw Kohl and motioned for him to join them. Kohl hadn't talked to Jack since he began work at the Purple Onion.

"Jack's got some news for you," Danny said. "Pull up a chair, and I'll get you some coffee."

Kohl's first thought was that the nasty Bill Gentry episode had caught up with him, which was no surprise. In fact, it was something he had expected. He was about to be fired.

But Jack Gengler smiled, which he found reassuring. Surely the manager would not offer a friendly smile in greeting just before giving him the axe. He took a chair at the table.

"How's it going, Kohl?" Jack inquired.

"No complaints. Leastwise none anybody would listen to. How's the world been treating you, Mr. Gengler?"

"Please, call me Jack. Mr. Gengler was my daddy."

"Fair enough. So how are things?"

"Oh, I can't say I have nothing to complain about, but things are going pretty good. But like my grandpa used to say, don't get cocky and try spittin' into the wind. That's one thing that can turn a good day bad real quick."

Kohl laughed. He was seeing a side of Jack Gengler he wasn't aware of.

"What I wanted to talk to you about isn't news so much as it is a proposition," Jack said. He paused while Danny put a cup in front of Kohl and poured coffee, then went on. "You've shown yourself to be a good and dependable worker, and it's no secret that you and Cara are keeping pretty close company. We could use you on the day shift, so I thought you might like to work the same schedule as she does. Would you like to make the switch?"

"Well, yeah, it would make me the happiest man in the world," Kohl answered. "And I know Cara would like it. It would make her life a lot simpler if we could come and go at the same time."

"Consider it done, then. Let me figure out the schedule for the women who work days, and I'll let you know when to start. In the meantime, don't let Danny work you too hard."

"Danny's pretty easy on me. And thanks very much, Jack."

Jack Gengler pushed his chair back and stood. "I need to be getting home," he said. "I'll see you fellows later."

Kohl waited until he was out of earshot before speaking to Danny, who was still standing. "If you had anything to do with that, I want you to know I appreciate it," he said.

"The idea started with Jack. All I did was tell him you are a hard worker and always show up when you're supposed to. I'm glad it's gonna work out good for you and Cara." Danny paused, as if he wanted to be especially careful about what he said next. "Before you start work I need to tell you something. Robert Hightower came in a couple of hours ago and told me what's going on with Sobeski. It's something you need to know."

"That sounds bad, Danny."

"Well, it sure as hell ain't good."

NINETEEN

THE DEEP COLD-room sink was full to the half-way level. Kohl turned on the hot water and doused the dirty dishes and tableware with soap. It would be hard to concentrate on the tedious chore of dishwashing when he felt an urgent need to warn Cara of Deputy Robert Hightower's report on Sobeski.

Who would have guessed, all those years ago, that little Bobby Hightower would grow up to be a lawman? He and Kohl had been playmates in the first grade, and even though they had had little contact in later years Kohl still considered him a friend. Bobby had been popular in high school. He was open and unpretentious, which made him likeable to other students, and the darkly handsome looks affected by his part Chippewa heritage apparently made him attractive to the girls. Kohl might have been jealous of the latter, but he was so enamored of Angie that he hardly was aware there were other girls in his school.

When Danny Connor told him what Deputy Hightower had done, Kohl's mind flashed back to the childhood friendship. He and Bobby had been inseparable through that otherwise unexceptional first school year. They had no contact over summer, though, and it was almost as if the friendship melted with the winter snow. Still, his first thought was that the deputy was motivated by lingering personal goodwill.

But Danny said friendship had nothing to do with it. He said Deputy Hightower had told him specifically that he was blowing the whistle on Sobeski because he felt it was his duty to do so. He said it was a personal motive driving his fellow deputy, not honest police work.

Robert Hightower told Danny that Sobeski had had a crush on Cara for almost as long as she'd been working at the Purple Onion, was furious that she had developed a relationship with Kohl, and was determined to find a way to make her pay. He said Sobeski probably spent half his time getting out Cara's name and description to police agencies all over the country and all but begging them to find something on her.

"He makes it sound like she's a known criminal and if they'll just check they may find she is on their wanted lists," Danny said. "Then he says there may be reward money involved, because he knows this will get people interested who otherwise wouldn't pay any attention."

Danny said Hightower explained that Sobeski believed Cara couldn't afford a lawyer and had no family to come to her assistance. Under those circumstances, it would be pretty easy for him to get her hauled off to another state and once that happened, even if she beat the charge in the end, he still would have got her away from Kohl.

Standing over the cold-room sink and replaying Danny's words in his mind, Kohl felt guilt as much as anger. He viewed Deputy Scott Sobeski as a despicable little creep, but this was not new. Until now he had assumed that he was Sobeski's only target. If Sobeski was out for Cara's blood, it was Kohl's fault.

While he was desperate to let her know what was going on, he hated to have to tell Cara enough detail for it all to make sense. *Then she would understand that it's all because of me.* And he might lose her, even if Sobeski never made a move. He felt guilty already. In the long run, though, guilt would hardly matter compared to the pain of a broken heart.

Even though his hands and arms were deep in the hot dishwater, Kohl was getting cold. His feet were freezing and the pain in his bad knee was getting worse. He checked to make sure there was enough of everything in the clean-dish racks to avoid a problem. The late hour assured that business out front had slowed, and there probably wouldn't be much demand for anything except cups and saucers. He saw no risk in leaving his work station briefly to get warm and went to the kitchen.

Danny Connor was nowhere in sight.

Kohl stood close to the hot stove, where much of the food served in the Purple Onion was cooked on the wide griddle. He'd been impressed at Danny's skill and productivity here. Danny was a formidable one-man force capable of carrying the full load of grill staffing during the night shift. For now, though, the stove and griddle mattered only because of their heat.

He'd been warming his hands over the griddle for a minute or so when Danny showed up.

"I thought you were lost or something," Kohl said. "I didn't think you ever left this spot unless you were waiting on a customer."

"Gotta get to the men's room once in a while," Danny Connor said. "Is it cold back there?"

"You could say that. I was about ready to switch jobs with you."

Danny laughed that big laugh. But then he turned serious again. "I've been worrying about Cara," he said. "Don't take this wrong, Kohl, but you probably know more about these things than I do. Could that slimy Sobeski actually cause her real trouble?"

"Yes. A scumbag cop can do real nasty stuff, and even if she didn't do anything there's no guarantee he can't hurt her. There's lots of guys wasting away behind bars after being railroaded by crooked cops. Women, too, I guess. Happens every day."

"Is there anything we can do?"

Danny's question was one Kohl had been agonizing over, himself. And he felt helpless. A determined cop with a grudge to settle was pretty nearly impossible to deal with.

"She's a sitting duck," he told Danny. "You can't even try to head off something you don't know is coming. He could pull out a case from anywhere. If we have any hope at all, it's Bobby."

A blast of cold air from the front of the room alerted them that the door had opened and someone had entered. Two men walked stiffly toward them.

"We'll talk more," Danny Connor said. "Right now I need to take care of these truckers."

Kohl went back to the cold-room and surveyed the work he still had to do. The water in the deep sink had cooled to lukewarm, and there were more dirty dishes than he'd thought. He drained the sink and refilled it with hot water and added an ample quantity of soap. There was enough work to keep him busy for an hour or so, especially if Danny brought more.

He didn't mind the work—would rather have enough to keep him busy, in fact—but he wanted more time to talk with Danny about Sobeski's foul campaign to find something on Cara. He thought it might be best that she didn't know, but he was open to Danny's thinking on this. And he wanted to discuss it before she arrived at the Purple Onion a few hours from now.

The realization that Sobeski actually might cause him to lose Cara had begun to weigh heavily on Kohl's mind. There no longer was any doubt that he loved Cara passionately. She was like a brilliant ray of sunshine after years of darkness, and he had commenced to think of the two of them, with Jake at their side, doing all the things they both had missed in life. Together. This had become his new vision of true happiness.

Danny Connor brought a tray of dirty dishes just as Kohl had almost finished what was in the sink. "The place is empty again," he said. "There's plenty of clean stuff on the racks. We can talk some more if you want to."

"Yeah, I want to. It's like you were reading my mind."

"Hey, I'm a talented guy, but mind-reading don't happen to be one of my talents. Let's get some coffee. You want breakfast?"

Kohl said he was ready to eat, and took a stool at the counter. Danny poured a cup of steaming coffee. "This ought to warm you all the way through," he said. "You want bacon or sausage with your eggs today?"

Kohl told him it didn't matter. All he really wanted was to talk some more about Sobeski and Cara. Danny said they could talk while he tended the griddle, and he'd have breakfast on the counter in the blink of an eye.

"I don't think we ought to tell her what's going on," Kohl said. "I could be wrong about that, though. What do you think?"

"I guess I think the same thing. Unless something happens that she needs to know, what's the use of worrying her?"

Two of the trucks that had been sitting in the parking lot for the last couple of hours had engines revving, and began to lumber toward the highway. Danny said both drivers had been sacked out in the sleeper cabs before coming in for breakfast, and both had ordered eggs with sausage, which was why Kohl was having sausage now.

"I had a couple of servings left in that open package in the refrigerator and you said you didn't care between sausage and bacon," he explained. "I don't like anything to go to waste, and anyway that's real good sausage. Wouldn't you say?"

"It's outstanding, Danny. Just like the fry-cook who fixed it for me. Now about Sobeski, how often does Bobby Hightower come in here?"

Danny got a big laugh out of Kohl's words of praise, genuine though factitiously worded. Danny was standing behind the counter, coffee cup in hand, his big belly shaking. He took a long drink of coffee before he answered.

"I s'pose we have to call him 'Robert' now, given that he's a deputy sheriff and all," he said. "Not a problem for me, since I don't remember ever calling him anything else. I don't know about during the day, but he doesn't come by very often at night. Least not that I can remember."

"But you got a phone number if you need to call him?"

"Well hell yes, Kohl. He's in the sheriff's department."

"Yeah, well. I didn't know if you'd call him on duty. Hard to see how he could talk openly right there where somebody might hear him. You know what I'm saying?"

"You got a good point," Danny replied. "But we better get back to work. I've got to get busy cleaning up. New crew will be coming in petty soon."

He went back to the griddle and began scraping it with a spatula. Kohl returned to the cold-room, but left the door open to allow such heat as would come in from the kitchen. He had just enough time to finish his work there before Cara showed up.

He felt better after talking more with Danny. Danny's word was good; Cara wouldn't know about Sobeski's outrageous intentions. *Unless he comes up with something!* I've got to get in touch with Bobby, Kohl thought. *He's right there. He would know if Sobeski's closing in.*

TWENTY

KOHL SAT FACING the back of the grill, impatient to see Cara come through the back door. He felt almost as if it had been days, not mere hours, since he'd seen her last. They would have to rush if she was to take him home and then get back to the Purple Onion on time. He hated the extra driving she had to do for him, especially in vicious winter weather like they were having now. With luck, his new work schedule would change all this and he was eager to tell her the good news.

And he missed Jake. As he'd told Cara recently, his attachment to that little dog had reached a point where he probably was as happy and excited to see Jake after they'd been separated for even a few hours as Jake was to see him. Cara said she might be jealous.

Kohl was surprised to feel a hand on his shoulder and even more surprised to hear the familiar voice of George Spencer.

"Good morning, Ernst," the newcomer said. "I wasn't sure if you'd be here."

"I just finished my shift. Cara should be here any minute to take me home. But I'm surprised to see you here, Mr. Spencer. Stop in to get some breakfast?"

"Actually, I did. Been thinking about it ever since you had breakfast with me the other day. Can I buy you breakfast? Then I'll give you a ride home and spare her the task."

Before Kohl could answer, he saw Cara coming through the back door. "Here she comes now," he said. "And thanks, but I've already eaten. I'd be glad to wait around while you eat, though."

George Spencer stepped aside as Kohl stood, waiting for Cara. She came to him, breaking into a little trot, and they greeted one another with a long embrace. Both men reached for a chair at the same time, ready to pull it out from the table for her. She threw up her hands and mimicked exasperation, then pulled out her own chair. Kohl contributed further confusion with an awkward attempt at introductions.

"We do what we can to help get your morning off to a smooth start," Mr. Spencer joked, as he and Kohl joined her at the table.

Kohl couldn't wait any longer to share his news. "Jack says we can work the same shift, Cara," he announced. "He has to work out a schedule first, but it could begin almost any day. I've been waiting to tell you."

"No kidding?" she said, and flashed a Cara smile. "Did you ask for that? I didn't."

"Nope. I wouldn't have had the nerve to ask for a change this soon. Jack and Danny had discussed it, I guess, and couldn't see any reason not do it. And Jack told me it's just so we can work together."

"Sounds like good news," Mr. Spencer said. "I told you Jack Gengler is a good man, Ernst."

"I have a feeling Danny had a lot to do with it," Kohl said. Then to Cara, "Mr. Spencer will take me home after he has breakfast, so you won't have to."

"Jake's in the Jeep, though," she said. "It'll be warm enough for him for a little while, but he oughtn't be out there too long. I'd bring him inside if I could, but Jack won't allow it. I guarantee you Jake's cleaner and better company than some of the truckers who come in here. I think Jack's a cat man, though."

"Hardly any reason anyone needs to choose between one animal and another," Mr. Spencer said, pushing his chair back from the table and standing. "They're all God's creatures as much as we are. I'll go sit someplace else so you two can talk. And I'll eat real fast. We don't want that dog to suffer from the cold. It is vicious out there this morning."

They waited until he had crossed the room before speaking, holding hands across the table, then both tried to talk at once. "You go first," Kohl said. "I'll be content to sit and listen. Forever."

"I'm afraid we don't have that much time, Sweetie. Did you miss me?"

"I miss you anytime our skin doesn't touch."

"Do you really think we will get to work together?"

"Yes," he told her firmly. "Yes, I trust Jack. He wouldn't have told me if there was any doubt it would work out, do you think?"

The hint of sparkle in Cara's eyes told him she was about to play Cara games with him. Reading Cara's eyes had become his own new game, and he had surprised himself by becoming very good at it. He knew better than to give himself too much credit; Cara's eyes were easy to read.

"What will happen when they find out how dangerous it is?" she said, pretending to be very concerned.

"Dangerous? How can it be dangerous?"

"Because when I'm out here waitin' and I know you're back there in the cold-room up to your elbows in dishwater and can't get away, you will be in danger, good-looking man!"

Kohl said nothing. He pushed his chair back, stood, and came around behind her. With his hands on her shoulders, he stooped and whispered in her ear, "You might not make it out alive, gypsy woman."

"You're a sweet-talker, too. Talk like that will get you anything you want."

They carried on this way, having fun as long as they could, until they saw Mr. Spencer coming toward them. Cara said as soon as she knew for sure he still was giving Kohl a ride home she'd go on back to the kitchen so as not to delay them. She was concerned about Jake out in the cold Jeep. Mr. Spencer apparently was thinking the same thing.

"I think we need to go before your dog gets too cold, Ernst," he said. And to Cara, "It was a pleasure to see you this morning. I'm going to take this man off your hands now, if you don't mind."

She pretended she would be grateful, but squeezed Kohl's hand and stood on tiptoes to kiss him softly on the cheek. "See you later, handsome man," she whispered. She turned back to Mr. Spencer and told him to please go on and get this man out of her sight.

The old man went straight to his truck while Kohl stopped by the Jeep to get Jake. The dog was shivering, but it was hard to tell how much of this was from the cold and how much from excitement. He eagerly accepted the offer of a lift by strong arms. Especially the strong arms of his favorite being on the face of the earth.

Once they were situated in his truck, Mr. Spencer posed a direct question. "So you have taken up with that Cara?"

"I'm very much in love with her, Mr. Spencer."

"She's supposed to be a gypsy, as I understand it."

"Irish Traveler. She explained the difference to me."

George Spencer pursed his lips in a way Kohl took to mean disapproval. "Umm," he said, as if not sure what words to choose. Or maybe he'd chosen, but did not want to say them.

"She's a wonderful person," Kohl said. "She loves me too, and it just seems like we're meant to be together."

"I'd never dispute somebody else's choice in love, Ernst. As long as it's actually love and not mere physical attraction. Friendship with someone you've known almost forever can turn to love, and you're on pretty safe ground. You truly know this person. On the other hand, you see somebody new a few times and find them very desirable. This might turn out to be real love in the end, but it starts with physical attraction. When God gave us an innate desire to mate and reproduce, He set us up for all kinds of trouble."

"Meaning there's a big difference between love and sex, right?" Kohl suggested.

"In simplest terms, yes. And you have to be careful. Sometimes these people have things in their background you don't know about. By the time you find out, you're already in too deep. Know what I mean?"

His comment took Kohl by surprise. He'd never viewed Mr. Spencer as a prejudiced man, intolerant in any way. Did he deliberately intend to cast Cara as somehow different? Was it because she was a "gypsy," or did he mean women in general? Either way, he was stunned by what the old man said. He had idolized George Spencer as a youth and his respect and admiration had carried over into adulthood. In fact, he'd often wished he could mimic his old friend's understanding and acceptance of others.

"No, not really." He wanted to say more, but held back, hoping he had misunderstood.

"It's just that women with a past you know nothing about sometimes turn out to be different than you thought. I didn't mean to single out Cara. I like her, and I hope she stays true to the image you have of her. I think I just worry too much about you, son. Forget what I said, okay?"

They were coming close to the old Kohl house. George Spencer slowed down, apparently planning to stop. "I forgot to tell you," Kohl told him, "I'm staying with Cara right now. You know where her place is, I think."

"Sorry. I guess I should have understood that. How does old Jake here like it over there?"

Jake was sleeping soundly in the seat between them. Kohl reached down and scuffed his head. The dog moved slightly, then was still again. "You don't have much trouble sleeping, eh fellow?" he said softly. Then, to the old man, "Jake seems to do just fine anywhere I am, as long as there's plenty to eat. He's getting pretty cozy with Cara, too. Mr. Spencer, I truly can say I'm well on my way to being a happy man."

"Then I'm happy for you, Ernst."

"It still bothers me a lot when people treat me like I've got leprosy or something. I guess it was foolish of me to hope people could forgive and forget."

Kohl was looking at Mr. Spencer as he talked. He saw the jaw clench, the hands tighten on the steering wheel. He could not see, but sensed, a sudden change come over the old man. When George Spencer spoke, Kohl thought he detected a hint of coldness in his voice.

"An ugly man can't blame the mirror, son. If you march to the beat of your own drummer, you end up wherever the beat leads you. You killed a man, and you almost killed your mother. I might get by the first, but not the second one. No mother needs a black-hearted son like you turned out to be."

The words struck Kohl like a lightning bolt from a cloudless sky. After all the kindness Mr. Spencer had shown, this was the last thing he would have expected. He was hurt, and also bewildered. Was this a change in the old man's attitude, or was it a true reflection of the way he'd felt all along? He thought back to his first day home, the day Mr. Spencer caught up with him walking along Old Church Road and gave him a ride. He tried to remember the discussion of the front-page *Gazette* story on his release from The Pines. Mr. Spencer had not condemned the report. *"I suppose it's still big news,"* he said that day, and, *"Doc Harrell was highly thought of."*

He wanted to lash out at the old man, but at the same time he wanted to make him understand. No matter how terrible the thing he did twenty years ago, it was not because of a black heart. What he did was not intentional, and what he did was not what people thought he did.

"I need to tell you about that night," Kohl said. "The whole truth has never really come out."

"Alfred North Whitehead said there are no whole truths, only half-truths. And it's when we try to deal with half-truths like they were whole truths that the trouble begins. I've always admired Whitehead's way with words."

"And so you understand—"

"Son, every person's truth is whatever he thinks it is. There's no changing that."

They had arrived at Cara's trailer. Jake woke when the truck stopped, and he raised his head and yawned, struggled up to a standing position, and stepped with his two front feet onto Kohl's lap. He waited patiently for the two men to do something.

"Better get him in and feed him," Mr. Spencer said. "I may see you again at the Purple Onion one of the days. Meantime, stay warm!"

Kohl opened the door of the old GMC and slipped out without speaking. He lifted Jake out and closed the door. George Spencer waved and drove away.

The trailer was cold. Kohl left the door open for Jake, who stayed outside to take care of his own essentials. After a moment of searching he found the thermostat and set it to a higher temperature. Jake bounded through the door and ran to one end of the short hallway, then raced back and sat down in the middle of the kitchen floor.

Kohl got the dog fresh food and water, hurried to the shower, and in a matter of minutes was ready for bed. He opened Jake's room, then went directly to the larger bedroom on the opposite side of the small kitchen and living area.

The torment of Mr. Spencer's words still burned in his head. But the pillow smelled of Cara. His distress gave way to a mildly euphoric weariness and in a matter of minutes he slept soundly. If he dreamed he didn't remember the dreams when he woke several hours later to Cara's touch.

Standing beside the bed with no clothes, she might have been the dream he did not recall. He wanted her instantly. She clearly was of like mind. This time the primary driving force was not love, but an element more akin to primitive animal lust. Their response bordered on violence and was over quickly.

"Oh, that was good!" Cara exclaimed.

"Couldn't have said that better, myself."

"We do good work together, handsome man."

"Work? You call that work?"

Cara broke into a fit of giggles, and Kohl began laughing, too. Before they had finished, both had laughed so hard they were nearly breathless. Kohl turned on his side and raised himself on an elbow so that he was looking her in the eyes.

"I miss you fiercely when I'm here without you, gypsy woman," he said. "I hope Jack gets the schedule worked out soon so we can do the same shift. Did you hear any more about it today?"

"No. But I'm sure it's okay. Otherwise somebody would have told us, don't you think?"

"I hope so," he told her, then chuckled. "It feels good to have someone ask me what I think—especially you. Let's make a rule that at least once a day we each have to ask the other what we think about something. To be honest, there are lots of times I wonder what you think but don't ask, or can't ask because you're someplace else."

"I like that idea. But if we're going to be honest, handsome man, I need to tell you something, okay?"

"That scares me."

"I'm scared, too. If Sobeski digs deep enough, he might find out I'm wanted in Kentucky for stealing a car. But it's not—"

"Oh, damn, Cara. Car theft might be the worst crime you could've done, I mean except for big things like robbing a bank or killing somebody. Insurance companies keep pressure on the cops to catch car thieves so they don't have to pay out so much. That's one Sobeski might find."

Kohl felt like he'd just been stabbed in the back with a dagger. Through all the talk and worry about what Deputy Sobeski could do, he had refused to think Cara actually might have a serious criminal charge pending somewhere. Sobeski was dogged when it came to satisfying his own selfish interests. Finding her on a grand theft-auto wanted list probably wouldn't take him long.

"But I wanted to say, I didn't steal it," she protested. "It was my car. I just didn't have the paper work."

"Why didn't that get you off?"

Cara told him her story, and he had no reason to doubt it. She described her job as an all-around maid, housekeeper, chauffeur, and occasional cook for an old couple in Paducah. She worked for them for four years and they had come to treat her almost like part of the family. She loved her work and had come to feel very much at home in their grand old mansion in one of the city's old sections.

"Mr. Berry said I needed my own transportation, and when he bought a new car he gave me his old Mercedes," she explained. "There wasn't any paperwork. He said he'd still pay the insurance and get tags and all that, so it wouldn't cost me anything and I wouldn't have to worry about it."

"And he was a phony, right?"

Cara shook her head. "No, he was a good man," she said. "At least in the beginning. It was like I was his daughter. But Mrs. Berry had a minor stroke that changed her a whole lot. I'm not blaming her, but I could see what was happening. He started to treat me different. Always putting his hands on me and all that. Right in front of her, too. She was such a sweet old thing, and I felt so sorry for her."

The thought of a sex-hungry old man pawing Cara was hard for Kohl to take. He wanted to hear her story through to the end, but at the same time he was afraid to hear all the details. If she had given in to the old man's demands, even as a matter of self-preservation, he didn't want to know.

"What happened?" he asked meekly.

"I just got tired of it, especially knowing Mrs. Berry could see what was going on. I didn't want her to blame me, you know. I couldn't stand the old fool anymore. I told him if it didn't stop I was packing up my stuff and moving out."

Kohl could see in her face that this memory was painful. He took her in his arms. "I'm sorry," he said gently, holding her tight against him. "That shouldn't have happened. Nobody ought to have to put up with that."

"He tried to stop me, of course," she went on. "He offered to pay me a big salary and hinted that he'd share everything with me someday. Actually, I felt a little bit sorry for him in the beginning. But it got worse when I didn't go along with it. He started getting rough with me. One night he walked in while I was taking a bath and stood there playing with hisself."

She giggled, and Kohl supposed that telling the whole story her own way was easing some of her discomfort. This was the way he wanted to tell her his own truth about that night twenty years ago. He wanted her to know that he never intended to hurt anyone. He was not the evil person still reviled by those who would not forgive what they did not understand.

"You know what's funny?" Cara was saying. "That old geezer was hung like a bull buffalo! To tell you the truth, I've thought about it a few times since that night and wondered what might have happened if I'd let him do it."

Cara was being Cara again.

"But to be serious," she went on, "he disgusted me. I told him Mrs. Berry come to see me about this time some nights, and he ran like a scared rabbit. I got out of the tub and threw my things together and loaded them in the old Mercedes and took off. And I bet you can guess what happened, right?"

"He accused you of stealing his car."

"You got it. I took off down the road toward Nashville and I couldn't have been more than thirty miles down the road when I saw flashing lights in the mirror."

"And so you were charged with stealing your own car?" He could feel that she was more relaxed now. She leaned into him and lay her head on his shoulder

"Exactly. And you won't believe this, but old Mr. Berry came and bailed me out and took me back to Paducah. I guess he really thought I'd stay, because he sounded like he was going to drop the stealing charge. I went straight to the bus station and he followed me down there and said if I left town the police would have me locked up by dark. I just waved at him out the window when that bus pulled out of the station!"

"So you're actually not sure you were charged, right?"

"Well, I'd already been charged. You don't think he went back there and fixed it after I left, do you?"

She pushed him away to arms' length and turned her head back so she could look him in the eye. He detected a bit of the "What kind of fool are you?" glimmer he'd seen before. He pulled her back against him and squeezed tightly.

"You're right, as usual," he told her. "But I think we've covered your life of crime now, and it's time to move on to other things. I make no claim to being hung like a bull buffalo, but I've heard rumors that gypsy women like me well enough as I am."

TWENTY-ONE

IT WAS THREE days before Jack Gengler got his staff scheduling sorted out and told Kohl to come to work at the same time Cara did on Monday. He still would work two nights in between and then have the weekend off, but Cara was working Sunday. Kohl knew only one other person on the day shift, and that was Cindy. He'd talked with her a couple of times since the morning she got irritated with Cara for not starting work, and liked her well enough.

Danny Connor told him there were three fry-cooks who worked varied hours during the day. "You'll like two of 'em," he said, "but one of them is a real jerk." He refused to say which one, promising that Kohl would find out for himself the first time they worked together.

Danny also had a new complaint about Sam Rasmusan's ambitious plans for the Purple Onion. "He's gonna put everybody in uniforms!" he declared. "You know how many uniforms I'll have to have? Working over that griddle is a dirty, sweaty job."

"You think that will include dishwashers? We're out of sight back there in the cold-room. What difference would it make?"

"Alls I know is old Sam says this is going to be a first class place to eat, and that means a uniformed staff. What in hell do them truckers care about a uniformed staff?"

Danny appeared to be in a general mood to find fault, and kept on adding to the list of things he was not happy about. After a few more specifics, Kohl recognized that the real problem was Danny's home life. Danny was having some difficulties just now with both his wife and the kids. His family was a topic Danny Connor rarely talked about.

Kohl let him grumble a while longer, but when his complaints were reduced to insignificant little things like the size of catsup bottles, he interrupted. "How's your sex life these days, Danny?"

Danny Connor's face reddened.

"Sex life?" he said. "What's a sex life?"

Kohl laughed, grateful that his friend had taken his challenge with good humor. Danny laughed, too, just a big smile to begin with and then a belly-shaking howl. This was what Kohl had hoped for, not only as a measure of Danny's altering outlook on life but also as a tonic for his own disposition. A shot of Danny's big laugh always brightened his day.

Not that he had any particular complaints. Since he and Jake had moved in with Cara, his day-to-day existence had been undeniably more pleasant. Unlike Danny, his sex life had been like weeks in paradise. Jake was happy, too, and seeing Jake doing his love dance was a highlight of any day. Kohl still felt the sting of rejection from time to time, but he had come to expect it and so was less vulnerable.

The single biggest disappointment still was George Spencer. He had seen the old man twice since the day he made the provocative comments about women and labeled Kohl black-hearted, and on both occasions Mr. Spencer acted as if everything were normal between them. This one he was not able to put aside; Mr. Spencer had been too big a part of his life.

Back in the cold-room, Kohl quickly found that the lack of heat was going to make for a long night. He kept the dishwater as hot as he could stand it. Within an hour, though, his feet were so cold he was beginning to wish he could put them in the deep sink with the dirty dishes. He made sure he'd washed and loaded into the clean-dish racks some of everything—plates, bowls, glasses, cups, saucers, and silverware—and joined Danny Connor in the kitchen for a get-warm break.

Danny stood facing the counter and talking with Jim Endicott.

When Kohl recognized the trucker, he started to duck back into the cold-room. Common sense prevailed, though, and common sense told him he seriously needed to stand near the stove and get warm. His feet were so cold he could barely feel his toes. He was too close to the other two men to have any chance of slipping in unnoticed.

Jim Endicott apparently remembered him. He raised a hand in greeting and called for Kohl to come join in the conversation.

"I'm already tired of hearing about Danny's problems with his home life," he joked. "Let's talk about yours for a change."

Kohl was struck by a sense of mild revulsion. The last thing he wanted to hear was a derogatory comment about Cara. He was chagrined enough by the sight of Jim Endicott, always to be associated with his characterization of Cara as a magnet for truck drivers who otherwise might not be drawn to the Purple Onion. Nonetheless, he stepped up beside Danny and offered a hand in greeting.

"Afraid you'll get no stories from me until I get some hot coffee," Kohl said. And, turning to Danny, "You warned me about the temperatures back there, but I didn't take it too seriously. You were right!"

Danny was about to respond, but Jim Endicott was faster. "We're gonna have more than cold to worry about," he said. "From what I hear we'll be under a winter storm watch tomorrow. Looks like it could be a real blizzard."

Danny Connor turned away from Kohl to respond to the truck driver. "It would have to get pretty bad to worry an old road warrior like you, Jimbo."

"Hell, I'm from Tennessee," Jim Endicott declared. "There's nothing I hate worse than an icy interstate highway. I don't mean we don't get ice down there, but up here, once you get it, it never goes away! Nobody but a damned Eskimo would want to live up here."

"Well, I haven't seen any polar bears recently."

"Hey, Danny, seems like I only get by here in the late hours these days. That little gypsy gal still keeping things hot for you?"

Danny Connor turned to Kohl. "Would you check back there and see if we have a dozen or so number ten serving platters, please? We'll need 'em when the morning rush begins."

Kohl stepped back to the cold-room and pulled the door shut behind him. He was both grateful to Danny and curious as to how he answered Jim Endicott's question. There was no such thing as a number ten serving platter.

He drained some of the lukewarm dishwater from the deep sink and refilled it with hot water, added more soap, and plunged his hands back in to pick up a dirty plate. The water was too hot, almost scalding. Instead of pulling his hands out of the water, though, he held them there and felt the burn going into his skin. He kept his hands in the water as long as he could stand it.

He felt blindsided by Jim Endicott's reference of Cara, and frustrated because he hadn't expected it. This was "Full-throttle Jimbo," the man who said of Cara that a trucker would stop in the Purple Onion just hoping she would "stick a finger in his coffee." This was the only reason he knew who Jim Endicott was. It should have served as Kohl's marker, led him to expect the worst. His own small failures kept getting in the way.

But who was this man? Did he know appealing waitresses in every grill or coffee shop on every interstate highway he drove? Did he have a wife and family at home in Tennessee? And a dog? A dog like Jake? Kohl's irritation lessened with thoughts of Jake. Jake was his best friend. Jake was family. Jake never would betray him.

He ran cold water on his modestly burned hands until the sting was gone and the reddened skin had returned to its natural color. It still would be uncomfortable to plunge his hands back in hot water to wash dishes, so he began to tidy up the area and double-check the clean-dish racks. When he got cold he often remembered the day Jake showed up at the back door of the old house, starving and freezing. He could hardly bear an image of Jake suffering. Fortunately, he could quickly replace that image with pleasant recollections of Jake in his present surroundings, warm and well-fed.

Ten minutes or so later, Danny joined him in the cold-room, laughing hard.

"Did you find them number ten serving platters I needed?" he asked, and laughed even harder.

"All I could find were number twelves," Kohl said, willing as usual to play along with Danny Connor's games. "But I thought the number ten request was a slick way to get me out of the way. So Jimbo's still hung up on Cara, eh? I appreciate not having to listen in on his shit!"

"I cut it off right fast. You doin' okay back here? Endicott's gone, so if you want to come back on my side of the wall and get warm there's no reason not to."

Kohl welcomed the invitation. His feet were cold and his bad knee ached more than usual. He wanted to sit in a warm place and drink hot coffee. He was coming to understand that the Purple Onion was the one place where he could count on seeing friends. He'd almost forgotten the incident with Bill Gentry, and it had not been mentioned again in his presence.

He was a bit concerned about working the day shift, though. Daytime customers likely would include a great many more locals. Most of those who came in while he was working nights were over-the-road truck drivers, and even if they saw him they could not care less who he was or what he'd done in the past.

As they came into the kitchen, a minivan was parking at the front door. A couple and four children spilled out and rushed inside. Danny went to meet them, while Kohl poured himself hot coffee and straddled a stool at the counter.

Danny promptly returned to his place at the stove and began pouring pancake mixture in little puddles on the griddle. In what to Kohl looked almost instantaneous, he also had bacon and eggs frying on the other end of the hot surface. He had watched Danny in action often enough to know the pudgy fry-cook could manage all this with ease. Danny soon had things plated and ready to serve.

Kohl offered to help, but Danny waved him off. "Got it covered," he declared.

He watched with great interest as Danny put food and drink on the table for what Kohl assumed was a family. A family. He almost had forgotten there was such an institution. But with Cara and Jake to go back to, he almost felt like a family man, himself.

TWENTY-TWO

ON HER WAY to work Sunday morning, Cara dropped off Kohl and Jake at the old home place. He had felt guilty for virtually abandoning it during the few days he'd been living with her, but still was surprised at the deep emotions brought on merely by walking into the old kitchen again. Jake behaved like a lost child who'd just found his way home. He ran through the house as if he needed to make sure everything was there and in its proper place.

"Missed it, didn't you?" Kohl said when the dog finished its inspection and came back and sat down at his feet. "Well, I did, too."

The furnace had been set to keep the house just warm enough to prevent things from freezing, but not warm enough for comfort. Kohl remedied this, then went upstairs. Jake followed him and stayed close on his heels, as if afraid the two of them might be separated. Things on the second floor were as they should be.

It hurt to see his mother's room still completely empty, though it was a good deal warmer than the rooms downstairs. Jake felt the difference at once. He sat in the middle of the floor, and once satisfied that he'd been noticed he lay down and stretched out as if he had no intention of leaving any time soon. Given the dog's apparent contentment, Kohl was reluctant to leave the room.

He'd been remiss in not getting at least minimal furnishings for it. That was near the top of his list of things to do. Once he had a bed frame here he could bring the old mattress up from the living room. Of course, it was Cara's visits with the mattress where it was downstairs that had been a main factor in his not getting other things done. Who could have imagined that he would find a new love so quickly?

"You know what, Jake?" he said, "maybe God is on my side, after all. You came from nowhere, and now you're my best friend. And I knew Cara was something special when I saw her at the Purple Onion the first time I was there. What do you make of that, eh?"

He watched the sleeping dog almost as if he expected the animal to speak and answer his question. Then he went on, "Did I tell you this was my mother's room? May be a good thing our bed's still on the living room floor. A boy might be a little backward about having sex with a woman in his mother's room, you know?"

He sat on the bare floor and leaned back against the wall. Memories of his mother flooded his senses. The things he recalled most easily were summer things: his mother chasing butterflies among the flowers, his mother on hands and knees weeding the garden, his mother taking in and making a home for lost dogs and cats, his mother putting up flags and spreading the traditional July Fourth picnic fare under the trees in the back yard years after his father died.

She was still young, in his memories. She should have had a long, happy life ahead. But that was not to be. George Spencer's bitter words chorused through his mind. *"You killed a man, and you almost killed your mother. . . . No mother needs a black-hearted son like you . . . ."*

Kohl's pain was made worse by the realization that Mr. Spencer's charge was true. Or nearly so. Events leading to his horrific deed might mitigate the black-heart allusion, but events leading to his horrific deed still were unknown to the world at large. Only two people could tell this story. Besides Kohl, the other person was Angie. He doubted she ever had breathed a word of it to anyone, and even though he was ready to tell it now under the right circumstances, during his years behind bars he had steadfastly clung to his vow of silence on the subject. His only purpose was to protect Angie.

Countless times he'd asked himself whether Angie deserved the fidelity of his blind devotion. And every time the answer had been the same. It didn't matter whether she deserved it. It was his to give, and his love for Angie allowed for any level of sacrifice.

From the outset he had hurt for Angie—and for himself. When did he first come to understand the hurt inflicted on his mother? It had taken much too long. He'd been utterly selfish. Black-hearted? Maybe so.

Somewhere deep in whatever self-awareness he had, Kohl understood now that nothing really had changed. If he had to relive that night, the darkest night he hoped a human ever would have to endure, his unconditional love for Angie would prevail once again. It was the power of this love that led to the thing he did, and just as it happened twenty years ago, the power of this love still would prevail if it happened today.

And now he'd reignited a flame he had counted as extinguished by his love for Cara. There was no barrier to block images of Angie that flashed through his mind's eye. And he was back in another time, a time when the love between him and Angie surely was the most perfect love on the face of the earth. Life was good and the whole world was theirs. Darkness had been replaced by light. Sunshine had replaced the rain. This was their special gift and theirs was not to question, but to accept and be grateful.

Kohl, sitting on the floor in his mother's room, once again felt that perfect love. How could it ever have been cast aside like something ordinary? It was no more ordinary than the sun, the moon, and the stars in the heavens! And at this instant he understood at last that, no matter what had gone before, this perfect love he held in his heart for Angie was forever.

Jake's sudden stirring caught his attention and led him back to here and now. He pulled himself up to a standing position. Jake stood, too, but stayed in the middle of the room facing the door.

"Jake's looking good today," Kohl said loudly, as if addressing others in the room. "Jake's the smartest dog in Michigan. Look at the way his ears stand up when I speak. Jake's my dog, and I'm the luckiest man in the world!"

Jake wagged his tail, but did not look back.

Kohl laughed. "Looks like you're ready to move on," he said. "Let's get on back downstairs and see what kind of food we can rustle up. Okay, buddy?" Jake already was on his way.

Several days past, Cara had suggested stashing a few cans of dog food in the old house for occasions like this. They'd put a half-dozen cans in a kitchen cabinet and Kohl retrieved one now. Jakes bowl still sat in a corner on the kitchen floor. He soon had the food in the bowl and Jake gobbling it up almost frantically.

"Good heavens, little man," Kohl said, "you'd think we didn't feed you over at the other place. Don't choke yourself, you little pig!"

While the dog was occupied, Kohl went back outside and around to the front of the house to check the mailbox. Mr. Spencer had placed it, properly, at the side of the road with easy access to the driver of the daily mail van. This meant that Cara could pull up to it in the Jeep and check for mail any time they passed. Sometimes neither of them remembered this, and any mail delivered to the box lay there for a day or so.

A mailbox bearing his name and mail addressed to him still seemed unnatural to Kohl. He had no reason to expect personal mail until bills started to come in, but he'd been amazed at how quickly those who profited from compiling and selling mailing lists had managed to have his name and address in circulation. In less than two weeks, advertising in various forms had begun to arrive in his box.

He opened the box and drew out a half-dozen or so letters and cards and thumbed through them hurriedly to verify that they were the usual junk mail. One letter caught his attention and caused him a momentary rush of excitement. It had a California postmark. It had no return address and none of the traditional indicators of personal correspondence, but the mere idea of a letter from Ada caused his pulse to race.

He ripped open the envelope. Inside was a nicely presented sales appeal from a West Coast travel agency. Kohl's spirits, unusually high only minutes earlier, plunged to the lowest depths.

When Kohl and Cara arrived at the Purple Onion, Danny Connor met them at the door. Kohl knew he should have been gone by now, and this coupled with the apparent forlorn expression on Danny's face scared him. Something serious had happened. His first thought was that Danny may have had a visit from Deputy Sobeski, or maybe from Bobby Hightower. But Danny spoke before either he or Cara had a chance to say anything.

"I'm sorry, Kohl," Danny said. "There's been a big mix-up and it's my fault. There's an error in the schedule and you won't be able to work today. Georgette was already on——"

"Whoa! Is that all? I thought there was a death in the family or something, the way you looked. It's no biggie for me to take the day off."

Kohl assumed that his relief surely was visible to the other two, though he hoped it was not. He didn't want any mention of what he had expected Danny to say. Danny would understand, of course, but Cara was much too perceptive for them to get anything past her. Any reference to either Sobeski or Bobby Hightower would lead her to assume there was something she should be worried about. He didn't want that.

"But I really am sorry. I remembered your schedule wrong. It's such a nasty day out there, it would have been good to know you didn't have to come in."

"I had to come anyway," Cara reminded him. "It was kinda good to have a big, husky man riding along. You know, just in case."

"I'll be more than happy to sit around here and drink coffee all morning," Kohl said. "Appreciate your concern, though, Danny."

Danny Connor apologized again, said he needed to get home, and hurried out the back door.

Kohl had told the truth. He was tired, and happy not to work.

He had slept very little following the day spent in the old house, and such sleep as he'd had was filled with nightmares. Fuzzy depictions of Angie returned, building as they usually did to that single night of horror. At that point he woke, terribly depressed by the vicarious loss of all things that mattered. After that he lay awake worrying about Deputy Scott Sobeski and the possibility that Cara faced auto theft charges in Kentucky. At some point, afraid his tossing and turning would wake Cara, he got up and went to the kitchen. Jake came out of the small bedroom and joined him.

Although both he and Cara had looked forward to their first day of working together, he would be content not to have to be on his feet all day. He hoped he'd made this clear to Danny Connor.

Cara went to work when the first patrons entered the grill, and Kohl got himself a cup of hot coffee and went to a table in a back corner where he felt sufficiently out of the way. From here, he could watch Cara at work and she could join him if there was a slack period that left her free.

He also was in a good position from which to watch customers come and go through the front entrance. And the next person to enter was Tay. The big truck driver saw Kohl at once, and came straight to his table. He clapped his gloved hands together for warmth, but his smile was big as ever.

They talked like old friends while Tay hurriedly ate breakfast. He said he wanted to get back on the road quickly because the weather probably was going to get worse and he had a load of hardware to deliver in Gaylord.

"Like I told you before," Tay said as he pushed back his chair and stood, "if you've got the time I'd be real glad to have you ride along with me. I can have you home before dark."

Kohl made an impulsive decision. He would go. He crossed the room to tell Cara, and he and the big driver left the grill together, talking as they went, looking for all the world like a pair of drivers typically seen at the Purple Onion.

It was snowing hard, the snow driven into their faces by a strong wind from the northwest. The parking lot was getting icy in spots.

"There she is," Tay said, "and I can guarantee she'll be nice and warm inside."

TWENTY-THREE

THE BIG TRUCK sat at the far edge of the parking lot, running lights ablaze and its powerful diesel engine idling smoothly. Tay unlocked the doors and Kohl climbed up into the passenger seat in the plush cab. He felt as if he was surrounded by luxury. The truck's seating, upholstery, and interior trim in general surely would rival that of an expensive luxury automobile.

He twisted around to look into the sleeper compartment and could see that it matched those Cara described from her experience at the Ohio truck-cleaning business. There was a bed and a refrigerator, and on the wall at the foot of the bed was a small television set. The ceiling and walls were padded, making the cabin look comfortable and inviting.

"Damn, Tay," he said, "you're living the good life!"

"Oh, yeah. Peterbuilt. Nothing better on the road! It's not paid for yet but I'm getting there. Got a good deal on it from a dealer down in Muncie, Indiana, who was overstocked and had to move a bunch off his lot. Less than a hundred and fifty thousand miles on it and all the comforts of home."

Tay went through the mechanics necessary to get the big rig moving, and Kohl was impressed by the smoothness of his actions. Once on the highway, the big engine seemed to roar and relax intermittently as Tay went through the gears. Once it was settled at cruise speed, though, it was not nearly as noisy as Kohl had expected.

Soft rock music flowing from speakers overhead was too loud to allow normal conversation, but Tay quickly turned down the volume.

"What's it feel like over there?" Tay asked. "Is this your first ride in one of these big boys?"

"Second time. It's like another world up here."

"Oh, yeah. I remember my first ride. Then when I got over here in the driver's seat it was brand new all over again."

Kohl was intent on watching the road. The heavy snowfall virtually blocked the headlight beams before they reached far enough to give any sense that he actually was seeing what lay ahead. He nervously checked Tay to see if he could detect any sign of extraordinary concern, and saw none.

But there was a hint of unease when Tay spoke. "I'm sorry we don't have better weather for your travels," he said. "This one doesn't seem to have the makings of a fun trip. But we're in Michigan in the wintertime, after all. Bound to be a little more than frost on the pumpkins, I guess."

"You're used to it, though."

"Yeah, to a point. But I'd hate for it to get much worse, man."

Kohl wondered whether a day like this might affect Cara's view of trucking as a way they could make a living together. Cara was not easily deterred once she'd set out to do something. He could imagine her response—something like, "We'd only truck in the South, handsome man!" Cara would be Cara.

Tay was quiet, obviously paying careful attention to the road. Kohl wasn't sure whether he should talk. The last thing he wanted was to be a distraction.

After a time, Tay broke the silence. "I hate to bring up a sore point," he declared, "but how are things going on the get-back-to-life front we talked about?"

"Better, I guess. I pretty much know what's out there now, and try to just roll with it."

"That's the only way. Making any big plans?"

"I'd like to get into this trucking stuff. How do you do it? I mean, how do I learn to handle something like this?"

"The way I did it was to get a job with a trucking company," Tay said. "It seems like there's never enough drivers. Some companies will train you—even pay you while you learn to drive. Not all of them."

The snow was coming in heavy flakes now, wet and fragile, shattering like gigantic water drops when they hit the windshield. The accumulation was outpacing the wipers. A layer of sludge remained after the wiper blade swept across the glass, commencing to freeze despite the heat blasted against it from the truck's defrosters. Kohl was barely able to see the road ahead.

"Damn, Tay," he said. "I hope you can see better than I can."

"I can't. It's getting a little hairy. But I've seen a lot worse."

Kohl's anxiety, growing steadily for the last half hour, had deteriorated into outright fear. He felt that he was at the mercy of a collusion of elements he had no control over. The big Peterbuilt tractor, initially having struck him as an impregnable fortress that would prevail against all odds, had begun to feel more like a death trap. He was at the point where, if he could have, he might have opened the door and jumped out.

"I know, it's kind of scary from over on your side," Tay said, as if reading his mind. "Don't worry, Kohl. I'm still in control of this beast. Slow and steady until we come to someplace we can get off the road."

"Yeah, well. I hope that's not too far. Make me happy and tell me there's someplace right up ahead, okay?"

Tay laughed. "I haven't been able to read the mile markers since way back and I'm not sure exactly where we are," he said. "But there's an interchange not very far. I don't usually stop there, but this time I will. We can get inside somewhere and get some coffee and wait this mess out for a while. Sound good?"

Tay's laughter had not reassured Kohl the way it normally did. His calm words helped, but Kohl still wished he could be in another place, sitting in something immobile, surrounded by sounds less threatening than the roar of the big diesel engine and more reassuring than the increasingly muffled slap of the windshield wipers.

"If you said 'get inside,' it sounds good," Kohl said. "Nothing personal, but I can't say I'm having a lot of fun right now."

"Believe it or not, I've seen worse. Not a lot worse, maybe, but worse."

"And you survived."

"I'm still here. Just hang tight, man, we're going to be okay."

It was another twenty miles before they reached an interchange where they could get off the highway—twenty miles that, for Kohl, may as well have been through hell. Tay exited and piloted the big Peterbuilt around a circular ramp and, just beyond it, a truck stop where it looked as if dozens of other drivers already had taken refuge. The parking area was crowded with semis, their big diesels clattering at idle speed and running lights marking their presence in the heavy snowfall.

Tay had to park at the outer fringe of the area, so it was a long slog to the brightly lit café and coffee shop set back well behind multiple islands of fueling stations. Once inside the door, they found it crowded and noisy. To Kohl, though, it felt like a peaceful haven from the storm.

They found a table and soon had cups of steaming coffee.

"I have to tell you," Kohl said, "I was getting a little scared out there on the road. No offense."

"Yeah, I'm glad to be here, too. Hate to lose the time, though. I'm not making any money sitting here drinking coffee."

"Sorry about that. How much time you think you might lose?"

"Couple of hours, probably. The schedule's not too tight, though. I'll make it up somewhere on the route by skipping a couple of coffee-shop stops if I have to. We weren't on the road long enough for you feel it, but at a certain point you just can't sit there behind the wheel anymore. Biggest danger is going to sleep. Too many truckers take risks, but I'll always get off the road and crawl in that bed behind me."

Kohl had been looking about, comparing this spot with the Purple Onion. The most obvious similarity was that the clientele here also looked to be almost entirely truck drivers. The seating area was maybe three times as big as the Purple Onion's, and no doubt it was busier than normal because of the weather. There were four waitresses, all of them very busy.

"Tay, do you know a driver named Jim Endicott?" Kohl asked. The question came as an impulse; he had not been thinking about Cara.

"I don't think so, man. Who's he drive for? Or is he an independent like me?"

Kohl didn't know, and he hoped Tay wouldn't ask any more questions.

"What can you tell me about him? Maybe I just don't know his name."

Having brought Endicott's name into their conversation, Kohl felt obligated to tell him more. How could he generalize? "I don't know much about him," he said. "He seems to think a lot of drivers stop at the Purple Onion just to see one waitress."

"Ah, yes. That would be Cara. He's probably right. She's got a lot of sex appeal, I guess you'd say. But hell, you know that."

"Yes."

"Look, Kohl. Where drivers stop pretty much depends on their routes. If they drive a regular route, they stop at the places they hit at the right time, maybe halfway between one place and another. You know what I'm sayin'?"

"I get that. So it probably wouldn't be because of a waitress?"

Tay's big smile spread across his face, followed by an open-mouth laugh. "Not the reason they stop, because there's not that much difference," he said. "Truth is, you won't find many of these places without at least one gal that drivers find especially interesting. Let's just say there's more big tips earned in them sleeper cabs than there are by good table service."

Three hours later, with weather reports indicating no improvement in conditions to the north, Tay decided to go back to Detroit. There was nothing perishable in the load he was hauling, and he felt it too risky to go any farther. Snow plows would have been at work, he said, and the trip back shouldn't be too bad.

"Like some great general must have said somewhere, sometime, it's better to retreat than to get blown to bloody bits by a land mine," he said, and followed this with one of his big laughs. "And that's all I know or ever want to know about war!"

"Coward's way out," Kohl joked.

But he could not have been happier about Tay's decision. He'd seen all the hazardous road conditions he cared to, and he wanted to get back to the Purple Onion. He wanted to see Cara, and he wanted to be home with Jake. Maybe the storm was less vicious there, but he should be with them. They were family; it was his responsibility to shield them from peril.

TWENTY-FOUR

KOHL HAD EXPECTED to have a problem concentrating on his mundane responsibilities in the cold-room when Cara was at work in the Purple Onion dining room. It hadn't occurred to him that she actually would be a frequent visitor, bringing trays of dirty dishes to his work station. They'd quickly made a game of her visits.

His harrowing road trip with Tay had left him with a nagging anxiety about being separated from her, which as the day began made him all but giddy that they would be working the same shift for the first time. That happy disposition had been dampened a great deal the minute Gracen, Danny Connor's morning shift successor at the griddle, opened the cold-room door for him and he entered the dismal little annex where the grill's dishwashing had to be done.

He had learned from Danny that Sam Rasmusan's grand scheme for upgrading the Purple Onion included modernizing the cold-room. Most important, the owner wanted to install modern dishwashing machinery to replace the deep sinks. This seemed like a no-brainer to Kohl, but Danny was skeptical.

"The only way that's gonna happen is if the numbers tell him firing you and the other dishwashers will skinny the payroll enough to pay off the new stuff real quick," Danny declared. His guess was that rather than a long-term interest, Sam Rasmusan was looking for a quick turn-around sale of the Purple Onion at a good profit.

"Hey, good-looking man, got room in your nasty sink for this stuff?"

Kohl deliberately did not turn to look. "Sounds like the voice of a gypsy woman bringing me more work," he said.

Cara slid her tray onto the parking ledge before the deep sink. As soon as her hands were free, she turned and grabbed Kohl around the waist. "I need a hug, if that's the best I can get," she teased.

He obliged, and went her one better with a passionate kiss.

"I may have to hurry people up so I can get back here more often," she said. "Do you ever get a break? I know Jack don't care if we get off our feet and sit down at a table when we're not busy, but I'd hate for him to bust in here and think we were makin' out in the cold-room."

Kohl promised to take a break soon, and she gave him a quick kiss and went back to work. He felt rejuvenated. Having Cara in and out of the cold-room would make his hours pass faster. Then they'd be home. Together. And make love. And see Jake. And he was not surprised that, once Cara's company was assured, his thoughts turned to the dog. Jake was the one family member he hadn't seen all day.

———————————

Kohl's shift flew by exactly as he hoped it would. He took breaks and sat with Cara at a table in the back of the dining area when she was able to, had quick contact when she carried trays of dirty dishes to the cold-room, and in general felt as if they actually were together all day. Their shift was over almost before he knew it. Whether it was real or mere fantasy, he believed he was as fresh at the end as he had been at the beginning.

Once they had checked out, Cara asked if they could sit for a time and relax. Unlike Kohl, she was very tired. She really didn't want to go out into the bitter cold and start for home until she'd rested and had some hot coffee.

"Somebody said Old Church Road's pretty much iced over," she said. "There's a couple of places where it gets slick as owl shit."

This got a good laugh from Kohl, even though he was getting used to her colorful language. He liked to accuse her of "gypsy talk," and she always said she picked up words wherever she worked and much of the time this had been places where there were truck drivers and didn't he know that truck drivers came from all over the country and a lot of them didn't always talk nice? And so that just proved how smart she was, he'd tell her, and they might pretend they had been quarreling and had to make love to get over any hard feelings.

"It's always fun just setting and talking to you," he told her. "Maybe we could just stay here all afternoon and talk. You probably have a million gypsy stories I haven't heard."

"No way, handsome man. We've got to get home to look after Jake. I miss that rascally dog as much as you do." She was looking past him toward the front of the grill. "Here comes somebody you'll want to talk to," she said.

Kohl turned to look. A man wearing a police uniform of some kind was walking toward them. It had been more than twenty years, but he was confident that the man was Bobby Hightower.

Kohl stood and welcomed his old friend with a big smile and extended a hand as Deputy Hightower got close. "It's been a long time Bobby," he said. "God, it's good to see you, man."

Bobby Hightower smiled, but it was a reserved smile. Reserved was the way he remembered Bobby. They'd always said this was his Indian part, and they never could tell whether Bobby was offended by this or proud to have his Chippewa heritage acknowledged. All this was from the later years, in high school. When he and Bobby were best friends and playmates in the first grade, Kohl never noticed such things.

"I heard you were back, Ernst," Bobby Hightower said. "Sorry it took me so long to catch up with you." And turning to Cara, "How's my favorite waitress doing today?"

Cara offered her charming smile. "Doin' okay, deputy," she responded. "I just got off work, otherwise I'd take your order. Coffee's always hot!"

"No problem. I wouldn't have time to order, anyway. I just happened to be passing by and decided to stop in and see who's here. I need to get back on patrol."

He looked back at Kohl and Kohl said to him, "I'm glad you stopped in, Bobby. It's always nice to see a friend from the old days."

"Yeah, we were friends in the old days, Ernst. But those days are long gone. I'm a deputy sheriff now and you're a convicted felon, standing here only because of some soft-hearted women on the parole board who mistakenly believe a killer can be rehabilitated. We're not friends anymore."

Bobby Hightower started to walk away, but turned to offer one more word. "Everybody was crazy about Angie," he said. "Nobody's going to forget the hurt you caused her!"

Jake was beside himself with excitement when they got home to Cara's trailer, doing his love dance over and over. It was evident that he needed to go outside, but didn't want to leave. Kohl went to the door and Jake followed.

"Come on, I'll go out with you," Kohl told him, and they both slipped out quietly.

Cara was visibly upset when they came back in. "Look at what he's done," she demanded, pointing to deep scratches in the wood paneling on the inside of the door. "You know I rent this mansion, Kohl. The man's going to charge me for that."

Kohl hated seeing the damage, and was very much surprised. "I'm really sorry," he said. "I didn't think he'd do something like that. He's never done anything at the old house. Maybe he needed to get out and couldn't. You've not seen any mess on the floor anywhere?"

"I don't think it's that," she said, her tone greatly softened. "Poor baby just got lonely. We were both gone too long, don't you think? Come here, Jake, and let me snuggle."

Jake had been holding back since hearing her irritation. He apparently picked up the change in tone promptly. He ran to her and wrapped himself around her legs, his tail wagging furiously.

"When we go in tomorrow morning, we need to drop him off at the old house," Kohl said. "He has more space to run around in over there, and there's not much for him to damage if he does get put out about something. And again, I'm really sorry about this."

Cara reacted with her prettiest smile. Nothing Jake did ever could be too bad, she said. She'd heard Kohl announce many times that Jake was the smartest dog in Michigan, she said. And being that her handsome man was so smart himself, how could he be wrong about something like that?

Cara was being Cara again.

"You're sweet, gypsy woman," he told her. "And that's just one of the reasons I love you."

"Love me? You? Then what do you plan to do about it, good-lookin'? Leave your dog here and come on back to my tent and prove it to me!"

With that, she giggled and ran to her bedroom. Kohl followed. And Jake followed Kohl. It was good. Jake immediately went to sleep on the floor beside the bed, and once he'd finished proving his love Kohl felt like going to sleep, too. Cara, though, wanted to talk. She sat up, leaning against the pillows at the head of the bed, and waited for him to do the same.

"It's what that deputy said." She spoke softly. "I love you, Kohl. I know you're a good man. But I need to hear about Angie and what really happened. I need you to show me there's no meanness hid in your heart, you know, no rage that might come busting out when I least expect it. You keep saying you want to tell me, but you never have. You have to tell me your side of it. And I need you to tell me now."

"It's a long story. I'm not sure where to start."

"We got all the time in the world. And like they say, just start at the beginning."

TWENTY-FIVE

KOHL TOOK A deep breath and folded his arms across his chest. "I've wanted to tell you all this since the first time I saw you, Cara," he said. "I mean that. The first time you served me at the Purple Onion, some kind of funny sixth sense told me you'd understand. I've never doubted that, or tried to second guess myself."

Cara reached out to him, put a hand on his arm. "I'm glad you trust me," she said. "Danny told me all he knew about what happened. And he said he always felt there was more to it than people knew, even if he didn't doubt that you was guilty as sin."

"I was guilty as sin, just like he told you. I never pretended otherwise. What people didn't know was why it happened, why I did what I did. Why it happened doesn't make it any less my fault or make me any less guilty. But it shows I didn't do what I did because of meanness in my heart, like you said. I never told why it happened to save Angie the humiliation. Maybe she didn't deserve me protecting her like that, but I wanted to. That's something I won't ever know for sure."

"So you're telling me you kept this big secret all these years because you're a big hero who just wanted to protect little Angie? Don't feed me no shit, Kohl. Yeah, I want to hear your side, but I want the truth. Heroes don't do what you did, okay?"

A quick smile softened the pained expression that had marked Kohl's face. "I learned in Mr. Hilliard's world history class in high school about a thousand years ago that you're not a hero if you don't sacrifice something. I mean, you know, pay a price. It didn't cost me anything to keep my mouth shut about Angie. Telling everything I knew wouldn't have saved me from being found guilty, and probably wouldn't have saved me one week in the pen. Get my point?"

"Okay. You weren't heroic. That don't tell me much."

"I was crazy about Angie. We went to school together and played together when we were little kids. We used to go around holding hands. I guess we just liked each other that much and it didn't make any difference that I was a boy and she was a girl. That came later."

"Yeah, Kohl, I guess men are all the same. That came when she started to develop tits, right?"

"I didn't mean that. I meant we were just road dogs."

"Road dogs?"

"Sorry. Something else I picked up in the pen. It means guys who just like each other's company. You know, go work out together when they can. That kind of thing. We still thought we were just friends in high school, too, but when school ended for the summer and we didn't see each other every day we found out how much we missed each other. My mother and sisters and me went to the same church she did, but I was embarrassed to sit with her. We'd just barely have a chance to say hi and then we'd be gone. I hated Sundays more than anything. I didn't have a car, so I walked into town sometimes to see her. I didn't have any money, either, so we didn't go anywhere or do anything. We'd sit under an old cherry tree in her back yard and talk. I thought she was so smart. She knew so much and it didn't make any difference to her what we talked about."

"What about her mama and daddy? They didn't get in the way of your little chit-chats?"

"Her mama had some kind of cancer and died when Angie was little. Her daddy was always at work. He was the only dentist in town. I think he had to be in his office even at nights and weekends sometimes. Angie would go down there and help when he stayed late."

"So when school started again—"

"It was like everything was normal again. We saw each other every day. We'd eat lunch together and she'd walk with me to my bus. Whatever we could do to be together."

"Okay, I get it. You were high school sweethearts. Then you finished school. So what happened then? I know you want to tell the story of your whole damn lives, Kohl, and I understand why, kind of, but can't we get to the part that matters?"

Kohl felt a sudden tightening in his chest. He'd wanted to tell everything to Cara, but now that it actually was happening he found it much more difficult than he had expected. Her reaction so far hadn't been what he hoped it would. Her impatience was irritating. Maybe this was a mistake. Would she really understand when she heard what she had just called "the part that matters"? Didn't his love for Angie matter? If it didn't, how could he expect any sympathy when he told her about what happened that night? He was scared, afraid to say more, and bitterly disappointed. But he had vowed to tell the whole story and he would.

"Our mother got a better car after I finished school and my sisters and me got her old one. I got a job at the Dairy Queen and Angie went to work part-time in the dentist's office. Neither one of us made much money, but I had a car and we could go to movies and stuff. Having real dates was different. Other people got used to seeing us out together. But the truth is, we still had more fun just doing what we used to. More often than not we just went to her house."

Cara held up a hand, like a signal to stop. "I can see where this is going. I don't want to hear about the two of you making out in the shower or rolling and tumbling in little Angie's bed with her Teddy Bears, okay? Just tell me what happened. She got pregnant or something, right?"

"We didn't have sex."

"Kohl, you're lying to me. Alone in the house and you didn't have sex? No way."

"I thought Angie wasn't like that. I knew other girls from school that guys said were easy, but I didn't expect that from Angie. We were in love and serious about it. We talked some about getting married someday, but we hadn't made any actual plans. But she was so good—so pretty and so sweet—I really wanted to spend my life with her. There would be plenty of sex after we were married."

Cara looked him straight in the eyes, her demeanor somewhat softened from the impatience she had shown earlier. "I believe you," she said. "I knew there were guys like that, but the ones I saw were hardly ever that considerate. They were always trying to make out. Had their hands all over me, tried to get me unbuttoned, all that shit. That's hard, you know? Girls want sex, too, once they get hot. If you like some guy and let him play with your tits and stuff, pretty soon you're going to have a hard time not giving in."

Now it was Kohl who softened. This was the Cara he had hoped for and expected, the Cara who would understand.

"I can get to the part that matters now," he said flatly. "I had come to feel so much at home at her house that if the door wasn't locked I just let myself in. She'd be in the kitchen, or in the den reading or something, and I didn't need to bother her to come to the door. One afternoon—it was a Tuesday, a perfect spring day—the front door was not locked and I went in. I didn't see Angie anywhere and went back through the house. And I heard them, Cara. I couldn't believe it, didn't want to believe it . . . the bedroom door was open . . . they were naked on the bed . . . Angie and her father . . . I just stood there and watched and they didn't know I was there . . . ."

Cara gasped. She put a hand on Kohl's arm. "Oh, my dear god. My poor, sweet Kohl. I know what you are about to tell me. You loved a girl and put her on a pedestal like some kind of breakable princess and never touched her and all the time she was fucking her daddy. My poor Kohl. Honey, I'm so sorry. So very, very sorry."

"That part was easier to tell than I thought it would be. But of course there's more."

"I know, sweetie. You killed him, yes?"

"It wasn't like that. I didn't mean to hurt anybody."

Kohl went on to tell the rest of the story. He told in vivid detail how Angie saw him standing in the door, how she put a hand over her mouth to muffle a scream, how Angie's father, Dr. Harrell, got up from the bed and started toward him. He told her Angie lay on the bed crying almost hysterically. He told her he saw no venom in Dr. Harrell's eyes, only a look that the young Kohl saw to be one of sadness and confusion.

"I understand your hurt and anger," Cara said. "Anybody would have felt that way. But you didn't have to kill him. Did he attack you first? Did he just stand there naked and let you kill him without a fight? How did you do it? You didn't have a weapon, right?"

Kohl pulled himself up straighter on the bed. He took her hand in his and held it to his breast.

"I swear to God I don't know," he said. "I don't know what happened. I've blocked it from my mind. Doctors call it repressed memory. I studied up on it in the library at The Pines, such material as I could find. I didn't know what happened, and I didn't know there was such a thing. They say it's the brain's way of protecting us from memories that'd hurt so bad we couldn't stand it. I guess it keeps us from going crazy."

Cara sounded doubtful. "But you remember what happened right up to the time whatever happened, happened," she said. "Do you remember what happened after that?"

"Yes. Like it was yesterday."

He told her he went to Angie, probably angry about what he'd seen, but when he got to her his heart simply melted when he saw how much she hurt. He told her Angie finally stopped crying and crawled out of bed, pulling a sheet with her to hide her nakedness. And they went to her father, lying on the floor bleeding from a gash on his head. He told her Angie threw herself on her father and screamed that he was dead.

"Did she call the police?" Cara asked softly.

"No, not then. She said she wanted to save me, and that nobody ever could know what happened—you know, between her and her father. I promised her I would never tell."

Kohl went on to tell how they decided to drag Dr. Harrell's body into the shower and tell police he fell and hit his head and he was dead when they found him. He told how they frantically tried to clean the blood off the carpet and thought they had been successful. He told her Angie got dressed, and they made up a story that they had been outside and didn't even know her father was home from the dental office.

"We thought we'd covered all the bases," he said. "I told Angie I would protect her secret as long as I lived, and we rehearsed our story one more time and then she called the police."

Kohl was emotionally drained, but determined to tell her everything. As always, Cara asked the right questions to keep him on track. He could see in her eyes that this was painful for her, too, but he knew she would stay with it until she was confident she knew the full story.

"What caught you up?"

"We turned on the water in the shower and left it running. A very perceptive detective wondered why the good doctor would have started to get out of the shower before turning it off."

He told her police were suspicious from the get-go. When they couldn't find traces of blood on the floor of the bathroom, they moved out into the adjacent bedroom and found blood on the carpet there almost immediately. Everyone knew Dr. Harrell was rich, he told Cara, and police figured what happened was a botched robbery. They knew about his and Angie's relationship and assumed they would lie for each other. Angie had the best lawyers in town, and even if she hadn't the prosecutors didn't want to smear the dentist's good name and had great sympathy for Angie.

"They said there was no direct evidence that Angie was involved in anything other than an attempted cover-up," Kohl told Cara. "And she fell under my bad influence to do that. They asked her a few simple questions and said she cooperated. I never got to talk to her again."

Kohl let the story end there, and Cara was satisfied. She no doubt assumed there was nothing else to tell.

He would not tell her how he and Angie looked into each other's eyes in the courtroom during his trial and how the love flowed between them. And Cara wouldn't hear how the two young lovers knew theirs was the perfect love, never ending. And she would not hear what was in his heart even now, as he told the story of that tragic night decades past.

He was certain of his love for Cara, but it was new and yet to be tested. Angie would hold her place forever as his first love, a love ripened from friendship and made perfect through togetherness over time. Perfect love never ended.

TWENTY-SIX

JAKE WAS EAGER to go. Once he understood that on this day he wasn't going to be abandoned when Kohl and Cara left the trailer, his excitement looked to be boundless. He ran to the door as Cara held it open, followed Kohl to the Jeep, and waited impatiently to be let inside. Kohl carried a bag of dog food, which he put behind the seat before he climbed in. Jake was alert in the back seat, watching out the window as if he wanted to be sure where they all were going.

The morning air was bitterly cold, but a bright sun just clearing the horizon and a cloudless sky offered promise of a better day. They had allowed extra time to stop by the old house and get Jake situated there before going on to the Purple Onion.

"God, I hope we don't have another blizzard coming," Cara said as she started the Jeep's cold engine. "Don't know about you, but I've had enough winter already."

Kohl agreed. "At least we'll be home," he answered. "No more road trips! I have to hand it to Tay, though. He's a cool guy under pressure. If I had to be out there again, I'd be glad to have him at the wheel."

Cara let the engine warm a few seconds, then turned the Jeep around and headed toward Old Church Road.

"Tay's a sweetheart. He probably was the first driver I got to know when I come to the Purple Onion."

It was apparent to Kohl that she was conflicted over his story, but she had offered no hint as to whether she viewed him in either a more positive or more negative light. He had mixed emotions, too. On one hand, he felt as though a burden had been lifted. He'd wanted to tell her all those things since that morning he first set eyes on her. But on the other, he felt both ashamed and embarrassed. How ridiculous he must have looked in Cara's eyes.

He had been overwhelmed with emotion, and did not really consider the full effect his story might have on her. Once again, looking back now, his motive had been remarkably selfish. He wanted Cara to know that it had not been in his heart to attack Dr. Harrell that night, but he wanted this for himself. He was not the black-hearted killer the law sent to prison without really knowing what happened.

But Cara had demanded to know. Bobby Hightower's words had left her confused and suspicious. He knew how Cara thought, how she reacted when she was uncertain. He could have anticipated her scathing indictment had she not found at least some minor cause for redemption in the previously untold part of his story: "You're a slimeball, Kohl. You got all hung up on a cute ass and couldn't handle it."

Her reaction, though, had been sympathetic. She took pity on him for the hurt and disappointment he would have felt. Or at least she had pretended to.

Preoccupied with his efforts to recall even the smallest clue Cara might have offered, Kohl was barely aware that they'd reached the old home place. She stopped the Jeep and opened her door and Jake bounded out before either of them had made a move. Kohl took the bag of dog food from behind the seat and followed Jake, who went straight to the kitchen door.

Cara came behind them. She still appeared to be somewhat subdued in spirit, Kohl thought, and this was a mood he hadn't seen in her before. There could be other reasons, but he was pretty sure his detailed report on that single worst day of his life had left her dejected and uncertain. She could not have missed his devotion to Angie.

Once inside the kitchen, Kohl poured a big bowl of food for Jake and left it and a pan of water sitting in the middle of the room. The dog, meanwhile, had raced through the house and back. As if in appreciation, he did a quick love dance.

"Who's the smartest, toughest dog there ever was?" Kohl began. "Jake, you say? Why, of course it's Jake. Look at the way his ears stand up when I speak! Look at—"

"We got to get moving," Cara called. She already had started for the door. "You be a good boy, Jake. We'll see you soon, okay?"

Back in the Jeep, she said nothing until they were driving up to the Purple Onion. "I'm still thinking about last night," she said then. "Please don't be mad, but it's gonna take me a while to sort things out. I didn't think it would bother me to hear you talk about your little high school love affair, but you don't sound like you've got over it. After what she did to you, Kohl, you'd have to be some kind of total idiot to still be carryin' a torch for her. Can't you see that?"

"I know that's the way it sounds to somebody else, but—"

"Damn it, Kohl, there ain't no 'buts' about it! Either you hate that girl, or you *are* some kind of freaking idiot! Men can be so damned stupid!"

He did not respond.

Kohl went straight to the cold-room without speaking to anyone in the grill. A heavy load of dirty tableware waited in the deep sink. This would be breakfast dishes piled up after the night man got off, he assumed, and he wondered who had replaced him in that slot. He wondered, too, whether Danny Connor and the new guy got along as well as he and Danny did. Although he was grateful to be on the same schedule now that Cara was, he would miss working with Danny.

But he was looking for a distraction from Cara's pronouncement just minutes earlier. Maybe he had misjudged her, after all. She was not the understanding and sympathetic woman he had marked her to be. That sixth sense that had come out of hiding the first time he came close to Cara was a fraud.

But then again, wasn't it possible that this all would blow over fast? Cara would be Cara again, and their companionship would be grounded in the same love it always had been. He was uncertain what to believe, and lacking confidence in his own ability to handle complex relationships with women. *Damn, Kohl. Maybe you are a complete idiot. And this has nothing to do with Angie.*

Mr. Spencer knew a lot about this kind of thing. As soon as he could arrange it, he would go see George Spencer and lay it all on the line. Mr. Spencer would be blunt, but Kohl would know what he thought the minute their discussion ended. And once he knew what Mr. Spencer thought, Kohl could ask him what he should do.

He felt better now that he had a plan of action. The last thing he wanted was to get people started taking sides. Angie or Cara? Cara or Angie? But come to think of it, this reflected his own dilemma. He'd thought he could live with both, but that apparently wouldn't happen.

He was about fifteen minutes into his work when Cara entered the cold-room with her first contribution to the deep sink. It looked to him as if the tray was piled unusually high, leading him to wonder if she had delayed as long as she could before facing him again.

"Busy out there this morning?" he asked.

"Pretty busy."

"You think Jake's okay alone today?"

"I don't see why not. Anyway, I got to get back to work. Tay's out there, in case you want to see him."

She headed for the door to the kitchen, with Kohl coming right behind. It took no time to spot Tay, his big laugh booming out from a corner table. Kohl went over to see him and was greeted like a long-lost brother.

"Want to go for another little truck ride this morning, Mr. Kohl?" Tay called out as Kohl approached.

"Only if you're headed for Florida, sir!"

The jovial truck driver stood and greeted him with an extended hand. He invited Kohl to sit and join him. Without being called on, Cara promptly brought hot coffee for Kohl, leaned in as she poured it, and kissed him on the cheek. "Don't let this nasty trucker talk you into another ride, sweetie," she said for both to hear. "He likes to take you up north where it gets cold and icy."

Kohl slipped an arm about her waist and pulled her close. "I do whatever this gypsy woman tells me to, Tay," he said. "She gives me lots of trouble if I don't." And whispering into her ear, "Love you, Cara. Thank you."

She went on to another table and Kohl turned back to Tay. "Cara being Cara," he said, to Tay's big smile.

Tay was about to answer, then nodded toward the front of the room. "I think that man's coming for you," he said.

Kohl swiveled in his chair to see Bobby Hightower headed toward them, walking fast. The deputy stopped at the table and looked directly at Kohl. "I don't have time to waste," he said. "Can I talk in front of this man?" indicating Tay.

"Yes. Tay's on our team. What's going on?"

"Get Cara over here, fast as you can."

Cara had seen Bobby Hightower and already was on her way. She was about to greet him as she walked up, but he began talking before she had a chance. He spoke with a note of urgency.

"Cara, I need to know. Did you ever live in Kentucky?"

Cara paled, and her voice all but cried out her fear. "Yes, I did. It was way back, though."

"Listen to me, Cara. And you, too, Kohl. I have to know, and I have to know right now. Sobeski's come up with a grand theft-auto from Paducah and, Cara, it has your name on it. Was it you?"

"Yes, it was me. But it was a mistake. Kohl can tell you. And it was a long time ago."

"That doesn't matter, unfortunately," Bobby Hightower told her, his voice suddenly softened. "I'm sorry, but Kentucky doesn't have a statute of limitations on crimes like that."

Kohl felt an icy chill run through his torso. The sensation was all too familiar. He was scared. His voice wavered as he demanded of the deputy, "What does this mean, Bobby? You've got to tell us."

"That's why I'm here, Ernst. We need to move fast. Cara, unless you can afford a high-priced lawyer or have some kind of political pull in Kentucky, they'll almost certainly convict you. You could get a stiff prison sentence. You never heard this from me, but if I were you I'd make a run for it. Right now. Once Sobeski gets here there's no way out."

Cara burst into tears, her body soon shaking with her sobs. She turned to Kohl and they embraced tightly, his arms around her like a protective shield. "What am I going to do?" she pleaded. "I love you, sweet man. I just found you. I can't leave you."

Kohl was crying, too. "You have to go," he said. "You have to go now, before Sobeski gets back. We won't be apart for long, but you have to go."

"But they'd know my old Jeep and—"

"Forget the Jeep," Tay demanded. "You can ride with me and disappear from the face of the earth. Come on! We've gotta get out of here!"

She clung to Kohl for an instant longer, until he pushed her away. "You have to go now," he said. And to Tay, "Take good care of this gypsy woman, won't you."

"Don't worry about it!" Tay answered. "She's spent time in my hut-on-wheels before. I know how to take care of her." He reached for Cara's hand and pulled her forward. "Let's get moving." He all but dragged her toward the door.

She looked back at Kohl, pain vivid in her eyes. "I'll let Danny know where to find me, sweetie. Promise me . . ."

Tay pulled her through the door before she could finish what she wanted to say.

TWENTY-SEVEN

KOHL CLASPED BOBBY Hightower's hand and thanked him profusely, speaking from his heart. "I'll never forget this," he promised. "You were a good friend, Bobby, and you're a good man. I'm sorry I disappointed you."

There were tears in his eyes, and there were tears in Bobby's eyes when he replied. "You're still my friend, Ernst. The kind of closeness we had as kids doesn't go away. But you better get moving, too. Sobeski's no doubt on his way."

Kohl said nothing more, not to Bobby Hightower and not to anyone else. He grabbed his coat from the back and rushed out of the Purple Onion and onto Old Church Road. The wind lashed his face with tiny ice pellets and the surface he walked on was ice-slickened and hazardous. He was conscious of none of these things, and he did not notice the pain in his bad knee. He walked hard, almost at a run.

His only thought was to get home to Jake. Jake was his best friend, and Jake was family. Jake would never betray him.

Too many thoughts ran through his mind, jumbled and contorted, run together until he no longer could separate one from another. *Three great loves, Mr. Spencer said. Angie, my first love and my perfect love. I was wrong. Perfect love doesn't last forever. And Cara was my last love.* Tay's words, too. *"More big tips earned in sleeper cabs than by good table service." "She's spent time in my hut-on-wheels before."*

He stumbled along the edge of the road, making himself clear of the traffic lane in favor of an oncoming car. With his head down, surveying the icy surface of the road as he walked, he did not see the various appendages that marked it as a police vehicle. Even when the car stopped, he didn't look up.

But there was no mistaking the voice.

"Better be careful out here in weather like this, Kohl. You could get run over."

"You're the only car I'll see, Sobeski."

"Anyway, I'm the only one that matters right now. I've got some bad news for you. I warned you about keeping company with criminal types. Seems like your gypsy girlfriend has a grand theft-auto warrant hanging over her head in the Commonwealth of Kentucky. Did you know that?"

"You'd lie to your own mother, Sobeski."

"Better be careful with that smart mouth, Kohl. When I get that gypsy woman back to Kentucky and they bring formal charges, I think I might just make a case against you for hanging out with a known criminal. Wouldn't surprise me to see you back behind bars before the holidays. In case you've forgot, you're on parole."

Kohl was struggling to hold his temper. Deputy Scott Sobeski would like nothing better than to provoke him into even a minor display of threat or violence. He was determined to not let that happen.

"Well, I'm getting old," he said to Sobeski. "Us old folks tend to forget things like that sometimes."

"You know where your girlfriend is? Don't lie to me, Kohl!"

"I don't have a girlfriend. How could I know where she is?"

Deputy Sobeski shuffled in his seat, making ready to drive on. "I'll be seeing you around, so don't forget my pretty face," he said. "And don't worry, I'll find your girlfriend sooner or later."

Sobeski started to raise the car window, then stopped and added, like an afterthought, "I warned you about that mean dog of yours, didn't I? He tried to bite me this morning. Maybe you didn't take me seriously, but you will next time."

Kohl stood where he was as Sobeski drove away. When he moved, he was driven by sheer terror. Oblivious to ice and cold and bad knees, he broke into a run and refused to break his stride till he reached the old Kohl house where Jake would be waiting.

The back door had been kicked in and stood partially open. He pushed it to make the gap wider and went inside.

"Jake!" he called loudly. And again, "Jake! Jake! Where are you, buddy? Jake! Jake!"

Nothing moved inside the house.

He went outside again, and again called Jake's name. Still no response. Frantic now, he circled the back yard, around the old smokehouse and into the edges of the woods. "Jake! Jake! Come on Jake, I want to see you!" Hearing nothing, he went to the front.

Jake lay across the front step. There was a ragged trail of blood across the yard, coming out of the shrubs at the end of the house and leading to his body. There were three ragged bullet holes in his belly.

Kohl dropped down beside the dead animal and took its head in his hands. The body already was cold and stiff.

"Why in the name of God did he have to do it this way?" he sobbed. "I'm sorry, Jake. You never hurt anybody in your life. You didn't deserve this. He had no right to take it out on you. I'm so sorry. So very, very sorry. Forgive me, Jake, for getting you into this. You were the best friend I ever had. I just wish you'd had a better friend than me."

He sat and held the dog's head in his hands for a long while, stroking and petting as if the animal still lived.

"Who's the smartest, toughest dog there ever was? Jake, you say? Why, of course it's Jake. Look at the way his ears stand up . . ." He began to sob, softly at first and then violently, uncontrolled emotion taking control. He was unable to speak for a few minutes, then managed to choke out his words. "Look at the curl in his tail! Jake's the best dog ever to set foot in Michigan. And Jake's my buddy! And that makes old Kohl the luckiest man in the world."

He picked up the body and carried it around to the back of the house and laid it gently on the ice-encrusted grass. He went inside and took his axe from the kitchen cupboard, where he had stored it for Jake's safety, and went back to the dog's body. The axe rang out sharply as he chopped at the frozen ground.

Once he'd managed to dig a shallow grave, he took Jake in his arms one more time, embraced him softly, then eased him into the frozen earth and scraped the dirt over him until nothing was visible. He found two broken pieces of flagstone half-buried near the house, chopped them loose with the axe, and placed them on top of the makeshift grave.

Back in the house, Kohl rummaged through the drawers of the dilapidated kitchen cabinets until he found the old butcher knife he'd used a couple of times to open cans. He shoved it in his belt, pulled on his coat, and crossed in front of the fireplace and went out through the front door. He left the door standing open and did not look back.

He passed the mailbox that bore his name and turned toward town on Old Church Road. He walked fast. He no longer was aware of the cold, barely conscious of the fact that this familiar pathway was the same road home that had filled his dreams for twenty years. No matter. He would not be coming back this way, ever again.

-END-

About the Author

Robert Hays has been a newspaper reporter, magazine editor, public relations writer, political campaign manager, and university professor and administrator. A native of Illinois, he taught in Texas and Missouri and retired in 2008 from a long journalism teaching career at the University of Illinois. He has spent a great deal of time in South Carolina, the home state of his wife, Mary, and was a member of the South Carolina Writers Workshop. His publications include academic journal and popular periodical articles and eleven books, including his collaborative work with General Oscar Koch, *G-2: Intelligence for Patton*. Robert and Mary live in Champaign, Illinois.

If you enjoyed this book, please consider leaving a review.

More from Robert Hays

Fiction:
Equinox and Other Stories
Blood on the Roses
The Baby River Angel
The Life and Death of Lizzie Morris
Circles in the Water

Nonfiction:
Patton's Oracle: Gen. Oscar Koch, as I Knew Him
Editorializing 'The Indian Problem': The New York Times on Native Americans, 1860-1900
A Race at Bay
State Science in Illinois
G-2: Intelligence for Patton (collaboration with General Oscar Koch)
Country Editor